I0565987

Tolstoy & the Checkout Girl

~ a collection of short stories ~

Lis Anna-Langston

Mapleton Press

Mapleton Press
South Carolina

Publisher's Note: This is a work of fiction. Names, characters, places, and incidents are a product of the author's imagination. Locales and public names are sometimes used for atmospheric purposes. Any resemblance to actual people, living or dead, or to businesses, companies, events, institutions, or locales is completely coincidental. The non-fiction pieces in this collection are noted and accurate.

Book Layout Design Glow Design Partners
Cover Design Pixel Studios
Cover Art Yvette Gilbert

Tolstoy & the Checkout Girl/ Lis Anna-Langston. – 2nd ed.
ISBN- 978-1-957730-01-1
ISBN- 978-1-957730-02-8
Printed in the United States of America
Library of Congress Number 2021914868

for Mark,
my everything.

CONTENTS

The End of the Century

Stuart was my favorite roommate. Once he discovered gin our apartment was a revolving door of busted romantic encounters. It was the summer of 1999. Stuart's band was on hiatus. Rumors of a breakup persisted. Prince played non-stop on every station.

This was during the brown rice, miso, P.J. Harvey phase of my life. The phase where I started eating nut butter and organic rice cakes. I'd decided chasing guys, swilling tequila and staying out all night were not good hobbies. I turned my attention to a search for meaning. As luck would have it there was a school for enlightenment in Central Florida. Because pretension knows no limits, the school was built in the style of a fancy grownup tree house and desperately overpriced. I signed up immediately. Stuart had an adventurous spirit and saw this as an opportunity to expand his social life. On evenings when I didn't have to work part time at VideoXpress I meditated to the deep, wholesome sounds of Deepak's voice and Stuart borrowed my car to go to the gay bar. That's how he found Floyd.

Floyd was a mess. He'd spent the last five years living with an ex-Menudo band member on South Beach. Ex-Menudo was a lush. So was Floyd. Originally from Indiana he'd spent the last few years slung up in a South Beach condo listening to his lover, ex-Menudo swearing in Spanish parading around in hot, pink, satin daisy dukes, crying on the cordless phone because he couldn't get his manager to book him any gigs. Proof that boy bands destroy lives. Floyd told me and Stuart everything about his former life, right down to the size of Ex-Menudo's member which impressed me tremendously but not Stuart because in conversations where size matters you don't want to be the competition. Floyd was nice in an awshucks corn field homegrown pass the strawberry jam kind of way. That is to say, when he didn't talk and I stared at his broad shouldered, dirty blonde, sapphire baby blues, he was mercilessly hot. When I found him in the kitchen rummaging through my hippie provisions I explained the health benefits of probiotics and bee pollen instead of rolling my eyes and locking myself in my room.

"My ex was a health food nut, too," Floyd informed.

I liked ex-Menudo even though he added Vodka to his smoothies in the morning and shaved his balls.

Three days later Floyd made a German Chocolate Cake from scratch with honey and whole grain flour to pander to my new hippie, crystal clutching diet. I wanted to marry him. As it turned out, his MeMaw on his mom's side was a baker. Stuart dragged in from B-Side Records with an armload of pre-releases and handed them out like candy. Since he'd been working constantly they decided to go out. That was fine. I had meditation and German Chocolate cake.

My Indiana Vestal Virgin.

I wanted to tell him how hot he'd look driving a tractor.

The phone rang in the middle of the night. I pulled my pillow over my head and went back to sleep. The next morning I found Floyd hunched over the breakfast bar, frowning, listening to the message.

"What's up, buttercup?" I asked casually, sprinkling bee pollen onto my fresh yogurt.

"My Ex says he's going to throw all of my stuff onto the street if I don't drive back this weekend and get it."

Stuart's lips pinched together. "Can't he wait?"

I shrugged, standing at the entrance to B-Side Records, listening to Madonna bounce and tumble out of the speakers. "He says ex-Menudo will throw everything out the window."

"Sheesh," Stuart groaned. "I do not like this."

I shrugged. "Floyd is worried about his Fatboy Slim collection."

As usual, Stuart's intuition was perfect. Floyd left driving a U-haul but did not return that night. Stuart paced the kitchen while I made brown rice and seaweed for my school potluck.

"Should I call?" he asked.

"He's a grown man," I said.

He stomped off to his room and turned on Coldplay.

Loud.

The live album.

Not a good sign.

Right about the time Stuart was about to have a nervous break-down Floyd zipped into the parking lot with a truck full of prissy Little Bo Peep furniture. I was dead center in the living room poised in Downward Facing Dog when the sliding glass door opened. A glowing, bronzed Floyd smiled at my ass and said, "Now there's the money shot, Adeline."

Then he sweet talked me into helping him unload.

"What's with all of the glass knobs and curly cues," I said, letting my fingers slide through the grooves of the dresser.

Floyd shrugged. "I picked it up for cheap after it was used for a set piece."

Stuart didn't care. His Indiana honey pie was back in central Florida with us.

That was all that mattered.

I joined a Yoga Studio. The teacher was a bossy, taut bitch who treated deep breathing like a form of tyranny.

The one person we had on evening shift at VideoXpress quit. It worked out because I was on break from the school of enlightenment. They called it a fortnight of mindfulness. Floyd was tired of sitting around waiting for everyone to get off work and offered to keep me company.

I hunched over a new stack of titles waiting to be logged into the system as Floyd cracked open little airplane bottles of booze and poured them into his Pepsi can. "Being bad can be especially good," Floyd said, adopting a preacher tone, wandering off to browse.

Half an hour later he popped fresh popcorn, bought sodas from the machine, pulled up a chair in front of the big screen TV and popped in Terminator.

"Um, I'm only watching French New Wave."

Floyd glanced back over his shoulder. "Whoops. Sorry, doll."

He prowled the aisles for four minutes then returned and popped in The Professional. Okay, Luc Besson. Close enough. Around 11PM the store became a ghost town. I pulled my chair next to Floyds and pretended to watch The Usual Suspects. But really I was sneaking glances at him, thinking how hot he'd look tossing bales of hay out of the back of a pickup.

He leaned over, whispering in my ear, "I could lock the door if you like."

I straightened up in my chair. "Why?"

He jerked a thumb toward the clock. "Because you closed fifteen minutes ago."

I slid back down in my chair, trying to be casual. "Oh, yeah. Okay."

At closing I had to count down the drawer and the adult video titles in the back.

"The pornos," I wailed.

"Come again?"

"Three of them are missing." Three empty cases had been stuffed back on the shelves. "I have to find these or pay for them if they come up missing on my shift."

Floyd picked up the plain, black cases, studying each one. "Why don't they have covers?"

"It's not allowed. We're not licensed or zoned to display adult entertainment. Only rent the titles."

Floyd looked at the titles on the spines. "Okay, here," he said, "you count down the drawer and I'll see if I can find these."

"Really?"

"Yes. Some pervert probably misplaced them," he winked.

Ten minutes later he returned with pep in his step. "Done. I found them and put them back in the cases."

"Really?"

"Yes, Adeline. Really."

Everything was fine until Floyd borrowed my car to go grocery shopping. Stuart appeared in my doorway looking grim. "Have you noticed Floyd acting strange?"

"I've noticed you acting strange."

He ignored my comment. "He's been locking things up in a briefcase."

"Consider this, maybe he's just happy to have a briefcase. Before he drove back to Miami he had nothing."

"I don't think so. He's humming this weird song lately. I can't place it."

"He is a unique and special snowflake."

Stuart snorted and walked off. I followed him into his bedroom. Floyd was a slob. His stuff was everywhere. Their room was crammed with a ridiculous amount of furniture. Stuart jerked open a file cabinet, rummaging around.

"That's a violation of privacy," I said, stepping closer so I could peer over his shoulder.

He turned around just so I could see him roll his eyes.

He snatched a briefcase out from behind the dresser like a stepchild, thrusting it at me with a pleading look. I sat down on the bed and tried several combinations. Floyd wasn't the smartest man on the planet. "What if he has a generic combination," I asked.

"Like what?"

I rolled the numbers into place. 1, 2, 3.

Click. Click.

The simplicity of it stunned me. I opened it up. It was empty except for three black VHS tapes. Stuart pushed the briefcase aside, uninterested.

I pulled it back onto my lap. All of the labels had been scratched off. "I think these are the tapes that were missing from work."

"What? Why would Floyd steal pornos?"

"To watch," I ventured.

That kicked him into gear. The fact that I might have to pony up a ton of cash to pay for missing videos did nothing for Stuart but the thought of competition was unbearable. He snatched the tapes out of my hand and marched into the living room. He jammed one of them into the VHS player.

A scene flashed onto the screen, flickered and adjusted. A barn, hay tossed on the ground, blue sky beyond the big wooden doors. And lo and behold, there was Floyd standing there with a shovel in his hand.

Stuart squealed. "Oh my god."

Apparently I wasn't the only one who thought Floyd would look hot on a tractor.

So, there he was glistening with sweat, top button of his jeans undone. Stuart and I waited absolutely breathless, and then the most horrible thing in the world happened.

A girl walked into the barn.

Huh?

Stuart moved closer to the screen like he was seeing things. I had no idea what to do. It was like watching a train wreck. There was bad flirting, the old I'm lost routine, then clothes fell to the ground and they were doing it.

Ramming his finger against the TV screen, Stuart yelled, "That's a girl. A girl. A girl. That cannot be a girl."

Denial is a funny thing.

"It's definitely a girl," I said.

Stuart reached for the rest of the tapes on the floor but I snatched them up quick. "This has to be a fluke. Put the next one in."

I squeezed them tight and shook my head. "These are old. Forget about them."

"Adeline, I'm having an Aerosmith moment."

"Shit. Hold on." I jammed the second tape into the player. It was already queued to the middle of the tape. The scene was full stride.

"Don't turn around," I said quickly.

"Why?"

"It's Floyd and two girls."

"What?" Stuart spun around, gawked at the tangled, naked bodies on the screen, grabbed his head and screamed. "Why is this happening to me?"

"I told you not to look."

"Gross. there's two of them."

"Yes, I mentioned that."

The three people in the video rolled around on white, girly, Little Bo Peep furniture. I didn't have to tell Stuart his bedroom was filled with furniture from a porn set. He knew it. Together our eyes fell on the last tape in my hands.

Stuart grabbed my arm. "Get the Bombay."

Tape number three. The horrifying mystery.

I was at the refrigerator, hand gripping the bottle of gin when I heard it. The look on Stuart's face confirmed my fear. The front door slammed shut.

"Hola, I have returned with provisions," Floyd yelled down the hall.

I wedged myself into the tiny space between the refrigerator and wall, hiding half of my body and all of the tapes.

Stuart leapt to attention. "Hi," he screeched, cleared his throat and said much more manly, "How are you?"

Floyd stopped in the hallway. "What are you doing?"

Violating your privacy, I thought.

Stuart went in for the quick save. "We were just about to make gin martinis."

"Without me?" he inquired.

"I know. I'm sorry," Stuart said, channeling his guilt.

"Well, then I came right on time. As usual."

I felt around next to the fridge for a plastic bag to hide the tapes.

Stuart offered, "I'll help you bring in the groceries."

A second later I heard them walk down the hall. Once the door shut I ran full speed to their bedroom, dropped the tapes into the briefcase, slammed it shut, spun the lock, shoved the case under the bed and stood up to run.

All without knowing what was on tape number three. I turned and smacked right into the open closet door. A searing pain shot through my nostrils. I stumbled into the hall, holding my nose.

Exactly three seconds later Floyd and Stuart walked in carrying grocery bags.

Floyd glanced over at me, brow furrowed. "Are you okay, Adeline?"

"What? Me?" I said, in this high-pitched nasal voice. "Yes. Why?"

"Your cheeks are flushed, your hair is a mess and you're holding your face."

I pulled my hand away from my face to touch my hair.

Floyd's jaw dropped open. "You're bleeding."

I reached for my nose. Stuart glared at me.

The phone rang. All three of us looked at each other. Floyd lowered his bags to the floor and walked to the phone. "Hello?"

He listened a minute, then held the receiver out for me. "It's for you, Adeline."

Stuart walked to his bedroom and slammed the door.

I picked up the phone and said hello. Talking made my nose burn.

"We got robbed," my slacker boss Conner blurted loudly into the phone.

I groaned. Better him than me. "That sucks."

"Yeah, I need you to come in."

My whole body slumped forward. "For what?"

"Because I've got to go down to the police station and deal with this crap." Conner hung up without saying goodbye. He wasn't really a goodbye kind of guy.

I hung up the phone and turned around. Floyd was in the kitchen setting bags of groceries on the counter.

"I have to go into work," I yelled.

"Do you want company?" Floyd yelled back.

Nick Cave's Murder Ballads blared from Stuart's bedroom. Ominous sign. Best not to leave Floyd alone.

"Yes." I yelled back.

When I walked down the hall to get my bag of crystals and my purse, Stuart flung his door open and pulled me inside. Little speckles of blood dotted his closet door. I frantically wiped them away with my hand. Music blared from the speakers. Stuart leaned in, whispering loudly in my ear, "Did you see his screen name?"

I nodded, whispering back, "Rod Biggers."

An attack of creepy shivers made Stuart's whole body tremble. "When you get to work, look up the name in the adult movie database."

"Stuart," I growled, low and intense, putting emphasis on every single letter of his name.

He flopped his hair to the side, rolled his eyes and said, "Come on, Adeline."

"You are playing with fire."

He put his hand on his hip. "Wouldn't you want to know?"

I lied. "No."

"Come on, please."

I held my ground. Finally I said, "I'll do it for three new albums of my choice and that Trent Reznor poster where he's wearing all black and looks like he's about to climb on top of my naked body and kiss my hot, hungry mouth."

"I thought you were practicing enlightenment."

"I gave up hot guys and booze because they were getting me nowhere. I will never give up Trent Reznor."

Stuart gripped my fingers tight and shook. I knew he was serious and as much as I wanted Trent tacked to the wall at the end of my bed watching me, I knew logging into the adult picture video database was wrong in every conceivable way.

I had to get Floyd out of there. Nick Cave would be followed by The Clash, then The Cramps and then The Gun Club. I wanted no part of that play list. I wiped blood off of my swollen nose, grabbed Floyd and left before Ship of Fools was the tune I'd have to hum.

Conner tapped a pack of cigarettes against his thigh in that totally annoying way and handed me a deposit bag.

"What's this for?"

"You have to make the drop at closing. We can't keep money in the store."

"What difference does it make? We already got robbed."

"I got robbed." He rammed his finger into his skinny chest. "Not you."

Jerk.

The store smelled like popcorn. Apocalypse Now played on the big screen. All in all, it was better than whatever was blasting from the speakers at home.

Floyd looked over at me. "Tonight feels a little weird."

"Yep."

The phone rang. I snatched it up. Stuart slurred, "He went to Miami to makeamore adult pictures, the skank."

"What?"

"I'ma watch the third tape. I saws him."

Culture Club belted out the chorus, "I know you'll miss me blind..." in the background.

"I'va gotta go. I found more stuffs."

"Stuart... wait."

He pressed the button on the cordless phone. One short, sharp beep and he was gone.

Floyd cocked his head. "Stuart is a real drag."

"No you don't," I yelled, pointing my finger in his face so quickly it actually frightened me. "You will not pick on him."

Floyd raised an eyebrow. "That was fierce, Adeline."

"Stop it. This is not a joke."

He leaned forward so slowly, so purposely that I reached for the counter. "Jokes aren't my specialty," he whispered.

His mouth was inches from mine. His breath smelled like red hots.

If I'd been meditating regularly like my book on awakening inner fire had insisted, I'd be more fully prepared. Instead, I closed my eyes and took a deep breath, trying to think of something to say.

Floyd's fingers lightly traced my cheek, up and over the fine bones of my nose. "You've got a black eye. It's very sexy."

I reached for a stack of titles to enter into the system. Instead I knocked over Floyd's diet coke. A dark stain splashed across his white tee shirt.

"Oh, god," I wailed.

Floyd stepped back and pulled the tee over his head, revealing his perfect, broad, eye candy chest.

It made me lightheaded.

"There are some employee tunics we're supposed to wear in the back. Hold on. Let me get one."

I walked quickly around the counter. Floyd followed me to the middle of the store, stopping in front of the screen. I ran to the back and returned thirty seconds later with an ugly tunic. I handed it over and was about to make a joke when he grabbed my hand. "Just say you're sorry."

I turned. Big mistake. Scenes from Apocalypse Now flashed across his bare chest.

"For what?"

He slipped his hands onto my hips and I squirmed. "When was the last time you rode dirty, bareback hit it and get it?"

A breath rushed into my throat and stopped. I couldn't get enough blood to my head. I felt woozy.

The doorbell went ding dong and I jerked my head around to see one of my regulars staring right at us.

"Don't mind me," he said smugly. "I'll be in the back."

Bleh.

I locked eyes with Floyd. "What was that?"

"What was what, doll?"

"That. What we just did."

"We didn't do anything."

I sucked in another breath. "But we..."

"Could have? Yes, but we didn't."

True. We did not. Okay. Find your center, Adeline. Find it fast. Deep breath.

Floyd laid his hand against my lower back. "You're always so in control. The perfect foods at the perfect time in the perfect mindset. What makes you come unglued? What do you want? What's your naughty little secret, Adeline?"

"My what?"

"Everyone has one. What's the one indiscretion you keep to yourself?"

Floyd slipped his hand down the back of my jeans and when I felt his fingers on my ass I crashed into his chest like a ship wreck. In one perfect action he lowered his lips onto mine and I melted.

You know that kiss you've always wanted?

Yeah, mine was interrupted a few minutes later by the customer in the back. He walked to the counter to check out. Or more appropriately, check Floyd out, giving him the old I think I've seen you on a tractor somewhere look. The customer pointed at Floyd, "You look really familiar."

"It's the tunic," Floyd said, pulling it over his head.

At exactly 1:48 AM we walked through the sliding glass door. The apartment was quiet. The soundtrack of Stuart's life had gone silent. In the middle of the living room floor, Floyd's briefcase was wide open with the three black tapes propped up next to a handwritten note that read:

I know who you are. I saw what you did.

Cold shivers gripped my body. Floyd stopped, looking down at the spectacle. He turned and looked over his shoulder at me. "Do you know anything about this, Adeline?"

I shook my head.

Stuart did not return. I called everyone he knew. B-Side records said he'd taken a brief leave of absence because his grandmother died. Except she'd been dead for four years so he was lying. It was just me.

All alone with a fresh tub of miso and lots of time to consider enlightenment. Real enlightenment. Real nonattachment. Real ways to avoid suffering.

Stuart appeared ten days before rent was due, sporting angry, unkempt patches of facial hair and his favorite Ramones t-shirt.

"I'm sorry I didn't call," he said, staring at the carpet.

"It's okay."

"Where did he go?"

I shrugged.

"Is he still here?"

"No. He left the night you set out the tapes."

"Did he say anything?"

I shook my head.

"Oh," he said.

And that was that.

Stuart sulked a little more than usual which would have been noticeable if he weren't so given to melancholy anyway. I hated seeing him plod around listening to Sinead O'Conner sing, "There is no other Troy for me to burn..." or worse, Nothing Compares 2 U. Ugh. In a way I missed Floyd just as much. I'd been equally taken with him.

One night after a particularly grueling test on Chakras I found myself thumbing aimlessly through new releases when I saw the name. Rod Biggers. I wanted to catch a glimmer of Floyd's dreamy eyes staring at me from the screen. Just for old times sake. Not a big deal.

At midnight I locked the doors, popped some corn and sat down for the adventures of Floyd. In the video he was a fireman, stripping out of his soot covered uniform to save a naked woman in a plush bed with animated flames licking the curtains. Seeing Floyd naked again drove some ancient primal desire of mine to the surface. I watched the entire video, then walked to the back for more. In the next video he sported a park ranger uniform and stumbled upon a naked girl sunbathing. Next he was a Doctor checking on his very hot patient. I squealed with delight. A visual postcard. I watched him try on all kinds of identities. Carnival worker. Doctor. Gas Station Attendant. Chef. Guy next door. But my favorite one of all was the Police Officer and how he pulled off his sunglasses and leaned into the car, saying "I'm going to have to write you a ticket for traveling so fast through my county. I like it slow and easy."

The turn of the century loomed larger. I didn't fall in love or back-pack across Europe. It was the summer I traded dreams for fantasies. I bought a new wardrobe. Denim jackets and strappy camis. The band took a vote and got back together. On New Year's Eve, during the last night of the 20th century, I went to a local bar to see Stuart perform. The lead singer had pleurisy and his grandma had taken him to the emergency room. It was the last gig of the century and the first big gig they'd booked since getting back together. I huddled with them in a cramped back room while they agonized over what to do.

The drummer was the first to make a call. "Let Adeline do it."

"Do what?" I said.

"Sing. You know all the songs. You live with Stuart."

After half a decade of all male music making they decided to put a girl out front. I was horrified by the very thought of it.

"What?" I croaked.

Stuart stepped forward. "You're right. Let's do it. You're the one who rehearses with me at home."

He grabbed my hand and opened the door at the same time.

"But I haven't said 'yes' yet," I pleaded.

"I know you can do this Adeline. Do it for me," Stuart said so con-fidently that it made me misty eyed.

I didn't have a single reason why I couldn't do it. Enlightenment evaded me. I was still working part time at the video store. I owed Stuart. Even if he didn't know it, I owed him for the night that Floyd removed his tunic and made me scream.

When the blue stage light fell across my face I was stricken with fear. Trying to pull myself together I latched onto the first thought that entered my mind. I imagined taking my clothes off in front of

Floyd that night. Stripping down bare. Surrendering right there in that dark video store with the front door locked. I imagined each song was one long striptease in front of Floyd and it worked. At the end of the first set we got a standing ovation.

A single bead of sweat rolled down Stuart's cheek as he glanced over at me and winked.

At the school for enlightenment my instructor Indigo Rainn liked to say, "You're only free once you surrender."

On that stage, at the end of the century, I understood that it's okay to let things happen, to lose control. That all good things in life come when least expected, when you're not owned by your expectations anymore. It all came to me in a sudden flash. In that single moment I understood Zen. Not as a far-fetched religious principle but as a tool for engaging in a deeper dialogue with myself. As a tool for getting real.

We played all night, into the next morning.

It was the end of the year.

The end of the century.

The beginning of all things good.

I dropped out of the school of enlightenment and went on tour.

Vegas Thunder

One of Vegas Thunder's earliest memories was of his mother, Adelle, standing in the front yard next to a gaggle of faded pink plastic flamingos waving her cigarette in the air, screaming the F-word at the mailman. By all estimation Adelle had slept with the ice cream man, the meter man, six Highway State Troopers, two park rangers, one mechanic, and two convicts before Vegas was five years old. He was privy to this info because his sister Hollywood, who was three years older, kept a list in her diary. The diary had hearts on the front and a key she instructed Vegas to swallow if their mama ever tried to get into it. Hollywood never listed names, only professions. Next to the words she'd draw little stick figures of the men if she liked them. If she didn't like the guy she'd draw him as a little penis with eyes.

Gritty sand from the front yard of the trailer park got into Vegas's bed at night, grinding against his skin, keeping him awake. It wasn't the only thing that kept him awake. The screaming did a good job, too. His mother screamed more than any person he'd ever known. It was how she talked, how she communicated. Her lines of logic were strung together by chain smoking, swearing and screaming. Her dark, emerald green eyes drew men in but it was her tits that made them stay. Everyone knew that. Those big hooters cost three months of overtime and she wore them with pride. She liked to show them to everyone and almost everyone wanted to see them. All that noise kept Vegas awake, too.

Part of his childhood was spent eating Coco Puffs, watching cartoons on the 13 inch television set teetering on top of a plant stand, while his mother leaned over the coffee pot topless, wearing her work uniform. A g-string. She'd stand there smoking a cigarette, stirring her coffee, oblivious to his presence. Some mornings he found himself standing on an upside down five gallon paint bucket flipping light switches while nothing happened. If his mother wasn't home he'd walk down the hall and wake Hollywood who always knew what to do. She'd dress them both in fancy outfits she'd lifted from Goodwill and they'd walk down to Miss Francine's place, eight trailers down. Miss Francine's was the last one at the end of the narrow, sandy lane. Her place was surrounded by trees, cool and quiet, and felt welcome on long days when their mother didn't pay the utility bill.

"Why can't we turn on the lights?" Vegas asked his sister.

Hollywood smoothed wispy hairs off his forehead and straitened the collar of his baby blue suit jacket. "It happens," she said. "Sometimes the switch don't work right." Then she clomped up the front porch steps to Miss Francine's, curled her small hand into a fist and knocked.

They always had to wait. Vegas had no idea how old Miss Francine was but she was definitely older than Santa Claus. After he shifted from foot to foot about a hundred times the door finally opened.

Miss Francine always smiled when she saw the two of them standing there. "Oh goodness," she'd say, "come on in." Then his sister and Miss Francine locked eyes like they had a secret language.

Hollywood knew what to say. "Miss Francine. We were wondering if you needed some company today. Maybe you need some chores done or jars opened or I can sweep if you like."

Her place smelled like the candy she kept in fancy glass dishes crammed on top of dainty tables. Sweet cinnamon candy, mints that melted on your tongue, sugar babies and salt water taffy. Francine herself smelled like Lily of the Valley perfume and talcum powder. Vegas knew the name because he'd smelled everything in her perfect pink bathroom. Glass apples full of soap paper sat on the back of the toilet. Vegas loved washing his hands with soap paper, loved how it disappeared completely under the running water, bubbles floating up like magic.

Miss Francine motioned to what she called her settee. "Well, I could sure use some company for lunch."

Those words were music to Vegas's ears. Miss Francine laid out a lunch spread fit for a king even if it did take half an hour. Pimiento cheese sandwiches with no crust, cream of celery soup, oyster crackers and soda pop with pie and ice cream for dessert. Later in the afternoon, when their mother's Ford Fairmont didn't appear in the driveway, Miss Francine loaded them into her 1976 Lincoln Continental and drove to the J&S Cafeteria.

The worst part about Miss Francine's was the Old Time Jesus Gospel. All that holy ghost business scared the crap out of Vegas. The idea that dead men were coming back made him hide under the covers at night. Francine knew all the words, to all of the songs, and made him hum along.

When the sun set and their mother still hadn't returned, Hollywood took his hand, thanked Miss Francine kindly and walked back to the darkest trailer on earth.

Convinced all that darkness would swallow them alive, he asked, "Why can't we just sleep at Miss Francine's?"

"Best not to wear out our welcome," Hollywood said, taking a deep breath. "Besides, I got some candles from the dollar store last week. We'll be okay."

And that was the thing. They were okay. Hollywood opened her toy box filled with things they needed like boxes of macaroni and cheese, candles, candy bars and a jar of change in case there was an emergency. When Vegas asked her how she'd gotten the idea for the box, she said, "A T.V. show on how to survive a disaster."

T.V. taught them everything. How to cook, wash clothes, trim hair, schedule appointments, order vitamins, grow rose bushes, and how to build a deck. Wherever their mother had failed, the T.V. had triumphed, so it was spooky when the power was out. But his sister knew how to fix these things. She took out her tape recorder that ran on batteries and they played Rock Star. Hollywood was really good at it. She dressed up in short dresses and sang loud enough for the neighbors to hear.

Later, she blew out the candles and tucked him into bed. Leaning over to kiss him on the forehead, she whispered, "Ten four, little buddy. Everything's A-okay."

Vegas asked, "Where's Mom?"

Hollywood fluffed his pillow, glancing up at the stained ceiling. "I think she must be working a double."

Vegas pictured his mother clomping out of the house, muttering, "It's a four titty night." This meant a double shift at the strip club. "Two titties, twice tonight," she'd say, letting the screen door slam shut behind her.

Working late, Vegas remembered, meant men in the house. He kept a mental list of likes and dislikes. Earl brought pizza. Reggie loaded everyone in his Chevy and drove to the drive-in joint for hot dogs and tater tots. Dominic brought bags of fruit that Hollywood fed to the raccoons at night. He did not like Jimmy and Johnny Hollister because they drank a lot of beer and made mama cry. Vegas preferred four titty nights. It was like a vacation and usually guaranteed no adults in the house until at least 4 AM.

In the mornings after four-titty nights, piles of beer cans and bottles were stacked and strewn around the trailer. Sometimes, well, often, their mother brought more than one other person home with her. On mornings like these, Hollywood dragged a big trash bag out from under her bed and raked the cans and bottles inside. When Tuesday came around they walked down to Rydell's trailer to borrow his wagon. Rydell was nice but had a stutter. None of the other kids played with him since mean old Johnny Stacks called him a fag. Hollywood said being a fag didn't make no difference to her because Rydell was nice, stutter and all.

So every week they loaded up all of the beer cans and bottles and walked four miles down country roads to the recycling center. Hollywood never complained about how far they had to go. She took the cash, said thank you and stuffed it deep in the purse Miss Francine gave her for her birthday. Then, they traced their path back down the same country roads, holding sweating hands in the summer or pulling their coats down over their fingers in the winter to keep warm.

And every week they faithfully returned Rydell's wagon without a scratch.

Hollywood had other moneymaking ventures. The most lucrative was what she called 'rustling cowboys'. It brought the most money but wasn't consistent like the cans and bottles. Cowboy rustling was when she got up really early and went out to the living room to see if Mama's date left their clothes on the floor. If they had, she pilfered change from every pocket, stole all of the dollar bills she could find and, occasionally, snatched a five.

"Cha-ching," she sang, counting the loot. "That's what they get for getting caught with their pants down."

She ripped the stuffing out of a gorilla in her toy box and hid the money inside. Once a week they walked down to the strip mall to eat at Rocco's Italian joint. Vegas ordered Ravioli and two root beers. His sister ate lasagna. Afterwards, they'd run down to the dollar store.

Sometimes at home the phone wouldn't ring for a day or two so Hollywood would pick up the receiver and listen for a dial tone. Sure enough, it was dead.

"Shit." Hollywood slammed the receiver down.

Vegas couldn't remember a time when she didn't say shit.

"Shit. Shit. Shit," she'd groan. "Mama's done it again."

On days when the phone was dead and the power was off, Vegas day-dreamed his daddy would ride up in a Cadillac and take them away. It never happened. Truthfully, the only thing he knew about his father was that he was in Las Vegas the night he slept with Vegas's mother. That's how he got his first name. Thunder came from his mother. Adelle Thunder. The gods knew something when they named her. Thunder, storm, hurricane. That was her. His mama. One mama. No daddy. One time Vegas asked Hollywood about his daddy. She looked at him hard and serious and said, "Your daddy could be any one of these men rolling in and out of here."

She was right. Better to focus on other things.

They filled their free time after school playing what Hollywood called pretend. "Okay we're going to pretend that I'm Gretal and you're Hansel and an evil witch is trying to cook us," she'd say. Their mother was always the evil witch scheming to shove them in an oven.

On two titty nights Hollywood would often clean the trailer. At nine years old Vegas was still too little to fool with plugs, too little to heave the two hundred pound vacuum cleaner across the old carpet, so he stood on a chair in the kitchen, and washed dishes. Hollywood was twelve and she bossed him around. He didn't mind as long as she vacuumed the floor and left him out of it. The vacuum was deafening.

He'd climb onto the counters, screaming, "Hurry up," every time she turned it on.

On the counter he acquainted himself with all of the appliances he never used. The toaster and hand-mixer only had one side that worked and like most things in the trailer was well on its way to being broken. The blender both fascinated and terrified him. It was an old, hulking contraption, made of metal and glass that took up most of the counter. It worked perfectly. Adelle used it to make daiquiris for breakfast.

Because their mother worked from 4pm until who the fuck knows, the trailer was a drama-free zone until she stumbled in. It was the two days she had off that made Vegas feel like he was going to lose his mind. Hollywood called these 'no titty nights' and they made themselves scarce by catching the bus out to the strip mall to spend cowboy rustling money. If they stayed out late enough Adelle was gone by the time the last bus dropped them at the entrance trailer park.

Thursday was the best night. Hollywood had been doing up Thursday nights as long as Vegas could remember, making him pinky swear to never tell a soul. She claimed if their mother found out she'd ruin it. After school, they'd go by the grocery store, then hide out at Miss Francine's until Adelle lurched out of the trailer park in her rusted Ford Fairmont.

Then they ran home at full speed to make appetizers and change clothes. Once everything was prepared they went to the living room and waited. The first show was Dynasty. Hollywood went nuts for Dynasty and bought all kinds of hats and purses from Goodwill. They spent the evening sipping ginger ale from mismatched wine glasses, pretending to be rich. The T.V. show lasted an hour and was plenty of time to get into character. After that show came Knot's Landing. During the commercial break they had to run to change clothes and pull the T.V. dinners from the oven.

Vegas usually ended up being the chauffer or the butler but he didn't mind. It was fun watching his sister tease her hair on top of her head, ordering him around with an English accent. For years they had Dynasty night and when it went off the air Vegas didn't mind because it became Miami Vice night. Any twelve year old boy could see the allure of Crockett and Tubbs. That's when Hollywood started sneaking clothes from their mother's closet. She'd collapse on the couch, pretending to have a coke problem. Since Vegas was taller and the only man in the house he could take his pick. He could be Crockett or a bad Columbian Drug Lord. Twice he arrested his sister and made her spend the entire hour in a pair of plastic handcuffs she bought at the dollar store. He liked forgetting about the rest of the world because by the time they started playing Miami Vice, Vegas knew their world had been crashing down around them for a long time.

Sometimes Vegas heard his sister, late at night, crying. He'd ask her what was wrong. Most of the time she said something like, "I've got a stomach ache," or "I'm okay."

"Is it something I said?" he asked.

She looked at him so sweetly that it made him smile, but then her face scrunched up tight and she cried harder, her tears strangely illuminated by the glow of the electric clock. He could see that little girl inside of her but on the outside she was a fifteen year old reaching for her pack of cigarettes.

It went on like that for years. She'd hunker down next to the window and smoke. Eventually, the tears and smoke drifted away.

Vegas had begun to notice how people stared at his family whenever he was forced to appear in public with his mother. The other mothers with their puffy sweatshirts and bouncy ponytails glared at Adelle in her skin tight, low cut shirts with her big hair plastered in place with a can of hairspray. Adelle was every mousy housewife's worst nightmare.

Miss Francine passed away in her sleep before the end of Vegas' Freshman year of high school. He sat on the plastic toilet with the door locked and cried. His hiding place was gone. He closed his eyes, burning the image of her dainty, birdlike hands into his mind. The night of her funeral he broke into her trailer and stole her bottle of Lily of the Valley perfume. For days he held the bottle to his nose, pushing back the fear that bore down into his chest, tightening, twisting, haunting. The world came into focus. Days weren't filled with make believe anymore. They were filled with the subtle reality that he was going to have to take care of himself soon.

At sixteen, he got caught one afternoon smoking out behind the auditorium during a pep rally. The only other person in detention that day was a tough looking boy the girls called Easy on the Eyes Eric. When the final bell rang Vegas walked out to the curb, lit a cigarette and started in the direction of home.

A few minutes later, a guy called out behind him, "Hey, you wanna ride?"

Vegas spun around to find Eric leaning against a sweet Camaro.

Vegas took a drag off his cigarette, shrugged. "Sure."

The guy stuck his hand out to shake. "Eric Lloyd."

"Vegas Thunder."

Eric's grip was tight. "I know who you are."

The inside of the Camaro was spacious with a shiny sheen like it had just been wiped down.

"So what have you heard?" Vegas asked, blowing smoke out the window.

Eric glanced over, gunning the engine at a red light. "That your sister slapped Monica Bukowski for calling her a slut."

Vegas nodded, matter-of-factly. "She knocked Bubitchski's tooth out."

"Nice. Monica's no virgin princess," he winked.

Vegas nodded, without answering. He still hadn't gotten around to having sex. Wild, brown hairs sprouted out around his balls. He'd stand in the plastic bathtub in the trailer, staring down at his changing body. He wasn't sure hair on his balls made him a man but he was pretty sure it meant he wasn't a kid anymore. Sex had been one constant hassle his entire life. He wasn't looking forward to the hassle it would bring his own.

Three blocks from the trailer park entrance there was a gas station. Shiny and new, it offered the perfect excuse to keep people from seeing where he lived. "Pull in there," Vegas pointed. "I'm almost outta smokes."

Eric cruised to a stop at the front door.

"You don't have to wait," Vegas said, climbing out.

"It's no problem."

With his hand on the door, Vegas paused, "It's just right around the corner."

"Exactly," Eric said, his knees bumping against the steering wheel. "It'll only take a minute to drop you off."

Backing away from the car, Vegas decided to drop it. Inside the gas station he grabbed a cherry pie and slipped it into his pocket as he rounded the corner of the only blind spot in the store. Then he paid for a pack of gum and left.

Adelle was in the front yard wearing a bikini top and a pair of cut off jeans when Eric turned onto the gravel lane that led to the trailer.

Just my luck, Vegas thought, getting out of the car fast.

Adelle perked up. "Hey," she yelled.

Vegas ignored her, trying to get inside and avoid whatever embarrassment she was about to dish out.

Eric rolled down his car window. "Hello, Mrs. Thunder."

Adelle squinted her eyes. "That's Ms. Thunder."

Eric shrugged, running his tongue over his lower lip. "My apologies."

"Listen, honey." She perched one hand on her hip. "I think the Ford is outta gas. My gage is broken, but it's been awhile, if you know what I mean." She leaned forward, winking.

"Hop in," Eric said. "I got a gas can in my trunk."

Eric gave a little wave as he drove off. Vegas stood on the cinder blocks, stunned. He could hear Hollywood talking on the phone on the other side of the cheap, metal door. Finally, he shook off the disbelief and walked inside.

The air smelled like cigarette butts and hard boiled eggs. Two empty packages of lunch meat were on the cracked Formica table. He pulled the cherry pie out of his pocket and went to hide.

Half an hour later he heard the deep rumble of the Camaro's engine. Peeking around the edge of the blanket tacked to his window, he saw Adelle staring straight at Eric's ass as he bent over, pouring gas into her tank.

Gross. He flopped back on his cot, listening to his sister clomp down the hall. A second later she pushed his door open, dragging the telephone.

"Who's the hottie out front?"

"Don't you recognize your own mother?" Vegas said, flatly.

Slapping him on the shoulder, she jerked the blanket back, peering out. "The guy, smartass. Who's the guy?"

"Some guy in detention with me today."

"God. He must have gotten in trouble for being smoking hot," she said, letting go of the blanket, backing up. "He goes to school with you? How old is he?"

"He's legal."

The next day, Eric was at the curb, waiting. "Come on. I'll give you a ride."

Vegas climbed inside.

"You want to hang out?" Eric asked.

Vegas shrugged. "Sure." He thought it was the least he could do after Eric banged his mom.

The squat brown house didn't look like much but it was clean with cool, air conditioned rooms that smelled like blooming magnolia flowers. Pictures of Jesus filled the walls. Two, quiet, older people sat in the living room watching a breathy televangelist promise salvation.

Eric stopped in the doorway, clearing his throat. A little, gray haired woman glanced over. "Oh, hello, dear."

"This is Vegas. We're gonna have some snacks and watch a movie."

"That's lovely. There are sandwiches in the refrigerator without the crust, just the way you like them."

Vegas looked around the Jesus hallway and whispered, "Are those your grandparents?" Eric pushed his bedroom door open with his motorcycle boot. "Nope. Those two old fuddy duddies are my parents. I was what you call a change of life baby. I have a brother seventeen years older than me."

Later, a little gray head poked into the room. "Would your friend like to stay for dinner?"

Eric looked to Vegas, who nodded.

Eric smiled big. "Sure. But only if he can lead us in evening prayer."

His mother clasped her hands together. "Oh, that will be lovely."

The gravy boat had the words Sea of Galilee printed on the side. The salt and pepper shakers were Joseph and Mary and stored in a manger. Jesus Saves was printed in big, block letters around the edge of the Lazy Susan. Vegas couldn't remember ever praying. Not real praying. His praying consisted of things like, Please, God, make her shut up and Please, God, don't let her barge in drunk. Beads of sweat popped out under his shirt. Totally unnerved, but ready to get it over with, he lowered his head and whispered, "Dear God, thank you for this great smelling food and all things Jesus. Amen. Sir."

"Well done," Eric clapped.

"Thanks," Vegas mumbled, not really caring if he really meant it or not as long as someone passed the mashed potatoes.

Three weeks later Vegas was slumped down in the beanbag hoping Eric would drop the subject and move on to another. "I don't know," he said, quietly.

Eric punched him in the arm. "Why are you so uptight?"

"I'm not."

"It's one hit of acid," Eric flopped down on his bed. "It's not going to make you jump off of a building. Haven't you ever smoked dope?"

Vegas shook his head. "I've got enough to deal with without being stoned."

Eric raised an eyebrow, "Being stoned makes it more fun."

"You say that because you live with sweet, old people who don't hear very well and go to bed at 9 PM."

"8:30," Eric corrected, rolling over. "Okay, look, we'll do it here on the weekend. That way, you won't have to deal with your mother or your sister."

Vegas reached for his soda on the snack tray. "My sister moved out. She's living with some guy."

"Is that a yes?"

"Okay," Vegas said, caving into peer pressure. "I'll do it."

The next day he got a hall pass from his Study Hall teacher so he could go to the library and do research for his English class. At one of the computer stations he pulled up a search engine and typed, LSD. Lysergic acid diethylamide popped onto the screen. He glanced over his shoulder then scrolled down the page. His sanity teetered close to the edge on a day to day basis. Watching the ground breathe for twelve hours was a lot. These were things to consider. Finally he pushed back from the computer. He was supposed to be working on a report on Longfellow, due in two days. He didn't get poetry but failing the report lumped him into a category with failures. Failures lumped him into a category with his mother. A fact that made his stomach churn.

A librarian pushed a cart in his direction. He closed the search engine on the screen and went looking for Longfellow. Standing in-between the asiles, staring up at rows of books, he could smell the cigarette smoke still lingering on his jean jacket. His yellow stained fingertips trailed along the spines of books. Inside the books were the words of people who'd once been alive.

Just like him.

The bell rang.

Quickly he grabbed a book of Longfellow's poetry and went to check out.

That weekend it became clear Eric was not going to take no for an answer. Little white squares of paper, as big as a pinky fingernail, lay on Eric's desk for Vegas to see. "Where did you get these?" Vegas asked.

"Some kid I used to ride the bus with in middle school. His brother sells it on the side."

Pushing a square with the tip of a pen, Vegas asked, "Have you taken it before?"

Eric raised an eyebrow. "What do you think?"

"What about your parents?"

"They'll be safe in bed by 8:30. If it gets intense we'll go out in the garage."

"What if it makes me sick?"

"Listen, stop being a freak. Put it on your tongue, close your eyes and lay back."

"How will I know if it's working?"

"Oh, you'll know."

On the count of three Vegas put his square on the tip of his tongue, watching Eric do the same. He expected it to taste bitter but there was no taste whatsoever. Convinced the tasteless square was a dud, he laid back, his head falling softly to the pillow and listened to the blissful peace of a normal house until he fell asleep.

His eyes popped open. Eric was standing in front of the television. Sweat beads glistened on his forehead. A wild, distant darkness filled his pupils. A Preacher on the T.V. was talking about everlasting salvation. Eric hugged himself tightly, swaying gently to organ music.

Vegas sat upright. The wall rushed away, then snapped back into place. That was weird, he thought. Eric let out a low moan, grabbed his pack of cigarettes and said, "I gotta smoke."

Swinging his legs over the edge of the bed, Vegas stood on wobbly knees, not wanting to be alone. In the hallway, two nightlights lit a path to the kitchen. Faces of Jesus watched. Vegas stopped. The white face of Jesus, illuminated in the dim light, tilted left, then right. The house was dark, quiet. Peeking around the corner of the living room Vegas waited for his eyes to adjust to the moonlight. Rays of light floated, luminescent, in the air, with sparkling edges. The plastic runner protecting the carpet creaked loudly under his bare feet. Jesus lit up the mantle, washed in blue moonlight. Vegas walked to the picture and stopped. The clear glass frame was like a window. Jesus was on the other side, staring back. A thundering train of silence roared through his head. Unknown territory. This world and that world. Clear glass. Jesus in the window. Boom Boom Boom beat a drum in his heart, so loud, so intense.

"Hello," he whispered.

Silence.

Trying to orient himself, he turned, glancing around the entire room. His eyes swept back to the photo. The world fell away again. Now he was standing on a black platform under golden rays of light. Jesus shifted on the other side of the window.

"Do you know who I am?" Vegas whispered.

Jesus nodded.

Vegas stepped closer, laying his palms on the mantle. A burst of warm, intense love shot through his chest. In slow motion Vegas tilted his head back, singing Michael row your boat ashore. "Hallelujah," Vegas whispered.

Jesus stepped back from the glass. His robe and sandals came into view. Vegas stared, his eyes burning. Tears swelled in his eyes, a river flooding it's banks. Drops fell down his cheeks. All of the water will rush out of me and I will be bones and dust, he thought.

Now Jesus was up close. Vegas touched the glass frame but his finger sunk through to the other side. Jesus touched the tip. "Yes," Vegas said. "At last."

Boom Boom Boom beat a drum in his heart.

"Pssst..."

"I'm right here," Vegas whispered.

"Pssst..."

Vegas turned toward the noise.

Eric stood in the doorway. "What are you doing?"

"Talking," Vegas whispered.

"Come on," Eric urged. "Let's go outside. I think I'm peaking."

The night was alive. Vegas waved his fingertips through the air, touching trails of light. A deep, cold silence hummed. The crunch of footsteps on the hard ground was loud. He looked down at his bare feet.

Eric pulled open the side door to the garage, and stepped inside, swallowed by darkness. A light flashed on overhead. Between dark and daylight. The Children's Hour, Vegas thought. From lamplight descending. Broad star. Laughing Allegra. They seem to be everywhere. Words cascaded through his mind. Poems by Longfellow he'd spent the night reading. A fellow named Long. A fellow named Long. Arabs folding their tents. Dreary days. Sad heart.

"The wind is never weary," Eric said.

Vegas looked over. "What?"

"That poem you're reciting. It's Longfellow."

"How do you know that?"

"My mother was an English teacher for thirty-two years."

Sometime later that morning Vegas woke, cramped in the beanbag on the floor of Eric's bedroom. Trying to focus, he looked around and saw Eric passed out on the bed. A deep, metal taste on his tongue made him go in search of something to drink. Mrs. Lloyd was making breakfast in the kitchen.

"Oh, sorry," Vegas said, rounding the corner, startling her.

"No need to worry," she said. "Now I have company for breakfast."

Trails of sunlight shimmered and danced like the streaks of light last night.

"Orange juice," she asked?

"Yes, please," he said quietly, hoping, praying, he wasn't acting strange.

Gently, she set a bowl of cream of wheat on the table. A pool of butter melted in the middle. The sugar bowl was in the center of the table. As he reached for it sadness pushed up hard into his throat and chest. He missed his sister terribly and hated living alone with their mother. Horrified, he tried to swallow back the loneliness but it flooded his eyes, washing over his cheeks. Every minute, of every year, caught up with him in that single instant. Unable to hide it, he tucked his chin into his chest and cried like a baby.

Slipping into her seat, Mrs. Lloyd patted his arm softly. "Is there something I can help you with?"

Not wanting to explain sixteen years of something he didn't even have words for, he whispered, "Longfellow. I have a paper due on Longfellow and if I don't turn it in, I'll fail the class."

Closing her eyes, Mrs. Lloyd nodded. She recited a line, "Be still, sad heart and cease repining; behind the clouds is the sun still shining." She paused. "Longfellow. Yes, I can help you with that."

Later that night Vegas climbed the cinder block steps, feeling thick, heavy. The day disappeared into dark edges rising up from the horizon. The smell of stale cigarette butts seeped through a crack below the trailer door. Light spilled out onto his face and hands as he jerked the door open. A deep dread burned in his throat as he stepped inside.

Adelle stumbled down the hall and stood in the doorway, wearing a long T-shirt. Her hair was a wild, prickly mess. Dark circles loomed under her eyes. Chipped red fingernail polish clung to her fingertips. Her bottom lip was swollen and bruised from god knows what.

After a moment she raised her eyes, letting them roam until they stopped on him. "Now that your sister is gone you're going to have to start pulling some weight around here," she said.

Avoiding eye contact, he spoke to the linoleum, "Sure."

"Hey," she growled.

Vegas bit his bottom lip and looked up.

Slinging powdered cleanser all over the kitchen, she screamed, "Clean the sink."

"I have homework."

Adelle laughed, deep and throaty. "That's a joke." She lumbered over, jamming her finger into his chest. "I bet you don't even go to school anymore. Really, what do you do now that that scheming sister of yours is gone?" The cracked Formica table jammed into the back of his legs. "What do you do?" She repeated, ramming her finger harder with each word.

"Nothing." He ducked his head to escape her sour breath. "I just go to school and hang out."

Tossing her head back, he could see crusted blood on her chin. "In all these years not one girl has come home with you. What's with you? You don't like girls? Maybe Rydell's been sa sa sa sa sa sucking you off in his wagon." A raw, mean intent flickered in her eyes as she mimicked Rydell's stutter. Her pupils were dark, black holes. Spit and blood spewed from her mouth.

He was about to tell her about how Rydell cared more about him and Hollywood than she ever did or would. His mouth dropped open to scream but the back of his hand was across her face before he realized what happened. Blood spurted from her bottom lip. Vegas grabbed her by the mouth, squeezing his fingers deep into her cheeks. "You'll shut up. That's what you'll do!"

Slapping him hard in the face, she screamed, "I'm calling Bud."

Vegas let go of his mother and ran for his room. He knew now he had to leave. The doors were too flimsy to keep her out. He heard her grab the phone. He knew he could take Adelle but he couldn't take Bud, the new redneck boyfriend. Bud was three times his size, mean and looking for a fight.

Vegas grabbed a duffel bag, shoving whatever he could find inside. He'd always known this day was coming. Heart pounding he grabbed the gorilla with money Hollywood had left him and stuffed it in his bag. Glancing down, he saw blood all over his hand. A wave of contempt slammed into him, bile rising in his throat. Unable to stop it, he leaned over, vomiting on the floor, desperately wiping the blood on the blanket he'd ripped from the window.

Down the hall, Adelle screamed, "You're dead meat. Bud is on his way!"

Vegas shoved faster. His hands shook violently. Bud lived about eight minutes away and was likely to make it in half the time. He jerked the window open and pushed the bag through, watching it fall to the ground, sending a plume of dust into the air. Then he climbed up on his bed, and slid one leg through, then the other. The window creaked horribly under his weight so he pushed off fast, landing on the ground, falling to his knees. He picked up his bag and ran. In the cold, still night he heard Bud's big rig rumbling down the road. The moon peeked out from behind the clouds, illuminating the path that led through the woods.

Boom Boom Boom beat a drum in his heart, so loud, so intense.

Later that night he sat on a creaky motel bed. He counted the money in the gorilla and called his sister.

"Arkansas? What are you doing in Arkansas?" Hollywood exclaimed.

"I left her."

"You got any money?"

"I got everything you taught me and the gorilla."

Her voice cracked. "How in the world did you get from South Carolina to Arkansas?"

"I ran to the bus station."

"What are you going to do?"

"I'll get a job. I'm almost eighteen. I can send you money, Hollywood."

A deep, full sigh enveloped the distance. "I know how to rustle cowboys, baby. I'll be fine."

He reached for the map of the United States sliding his finger across the country, stopping on the city of bright lights that shared his name.

"Hey, Vegas?" his sister said.

"Yeah."

"She was always like that. It wasn't you or me. It was her."

"Do you want me to come back and get you?"

So far away, he heard her hair swishing against the receiver as she shook her head. "No, baby. Not this time. You get back on that highway. When that bus pulls out of the station, look back and laugh."

Vegas sighed. "Ten four."

"Ten four, little brother."

He heard a click. The line went dead. Holding the phone close to his ear, the sound of his breath echoed so that he imagined she was still there, still hanging on the other end. A strange silence hovered in the wires. Slowly, he laid back on the bed, pretending to float. Turning his head he glanced out his motel window. The curtains were open in the middle. A stream of light cracked the darkness wide open. In the cool, silence he whispered the only line he remembered. "And the night shall be filled with music and the cares that infest the day shall fold their tents like the Arabs, and as silently steal away."

The Dollhouse

At Christmas time my mom and her boyfriend Dave liked to get really stoned and make strings of popcorn to go on the tree. This would go on for hours. This was the same year I begged for a chemistry set. The trend at the time was to give me dolls from all over the world. Dutch girl. Spanish girl. French girl. Yawn. I wrote my list and taped it to the refrigerator. I told everyone I could find.

Then...on Christmas morning I thundered down the hall to find...

Huh?

I looked everywhere for the chemistry set. There was a Swiss girl, a China girl and that...thing. It loomed over the other presents, with its creepy, freshly painted, empty rooms.

"Cotton, don't you like it?" my mother glared me into submission.

I stared. I scratched. "What else did I get?"

Since she didn't get the reaction out of me that she wanted she went to an after Christmas sale and bought her own dollhouse. Rich, deep colors, tiny fingernail sized tile, miniature claw footed bathtubs, and tiny ceramic cookware filled it to the brim. Mine sat in the corner. She bought a new marble table for hers. When she was done, she started in on mine again.

I watched my empty house fill with furniture I had not ordered. I begged for Magic Rocks, "Pleeeaaasse..."

"No."

"A new chemistry set?" New parents? Anything but that stupid dollhouse.

"No."

"Well, then what am I supposed to do with it?"

"You play with it."

"How?"

"You move the people around in the house. Like this..." she said, dragging the little rubber man over to the table to sit down for dinner.

"That's not very interesting."

"Oh, Cotton, use your imagination," she said, throwing the Rubber Man on the cobbled bathroom floor.

I wasn't making my point very well so I slept in the hall as protest. At 5 AM I woke to the sound of the bathroom door closing, then, "Cotton, you are so ungrateful."

"Is it time for cartoons?"

"No, get in bed."

I wasn't going without a fight. "I don't want to sleep with the evil, evil dollhouse."

"Do you know how much money we spent on that thing? The house alone cost Dave a thousand dollars."

"So. It's evil."

"Stop saying that."

"Well, it is. It's a haunted dollhouse."

"It is not."

"It is."

"I'm not going to argue with you. It stays."

Okay, but my rubber people weren't dull. They threw china, slammed doors, had affairs, ran away with pirates, returned from voyages overseas, collapsed in piles of sorrow, drank too much, developed acute paranoia, formulated theories on why their house seemed so small and why therapy wasn't helping them with the sensation that they were always being watched and although not entirely realistic, never once sat down for dinner. I took old Barbies and used it as a homeless shelter. The butler, Sam, developed a drinking problem. The oldest daughter, Sadie, slipped into a deep depression and disappeared for days in my sock drawer.

"Hank," Sadie would say, "you've simply got to help me. I've been wearing the same clothes my entire life."

She was constantly auditioning for parts on soap operas. She'd practice all day in the kitchen driving the hired help closer to the bottle. Angeline was the cook. No one knew anything about her except...

"Cotton."

"What?"

"Who are you talking to in there?"

"I'm not talking to anyone. It's the rubber people."

"Well, stop. It's creepy."

Then Sadie turned to Hank as he refilled the ice bucket. "Darling, don't you think it's strange that none of us remember anything before we came to live in this house. It's like we didn't exist," she whispered.

Sadie was a sharp one. Hank looked over, his eyes swimming in stolen bourbon. "Honey," he'd say, "let's just forget about it."

"Only because you can't remember, either," she slapped back.

Then she took a lover. But I didn't have any more rubber people so Sam had to double.

"Cotton, it's time for bed."

Then Sam stole the plastic Mercedes and ran away with a Barbie six inches taller than him because he couldn't take the stress. Barbie thought he was rich because he always wore a tuxedo.

In the meantime, my parents were trafficking loads of narcotics out of our basement. Men who didn't speak English carried boxes out to trucks. These people had no names, no identity, no past, no future. Sort of like the rubber people.

"Hank," Sadie slurred, "Hank, why don't we have a front yard, honey? I feel so confined. Honey, I feel like someone's watching us."

Sadie was going to have to go back on medication. They were huge pills of artificial sweetener I'd stolen from the kitchen cabinet. Hank left everyday saying that he was going to the office but he really spent his entire day in the windowsill.

"What a fake," Sadie exhaled.

"Cotton, it's time for your ballet lesson."

"But Sadie's waiting on a call from a TV producer."

"Don't worry about that."

Sam came back after a week. Barbie dumped him and kept the Mercedes. Penniless and rubber he returned, smelling like exhaust and cigarettes. Angeline poured him a stiff one.

"Cotton, come on."

"Oh, alright."

Later that night a bright light flashed in Hank's eyes. He bolted upright. "What was that?"

Sadie looked around in a daze and said, "Aliens."

I turned off my flashlight and went to bed amused.

"Cotton?"

"Yes?"

"Stop talking to yourself," my mother screamed at the top of her lungs.

The next day my mother curiously disappeared.

"She has a headache," Dave said. "She's resting."

"Where?"

"In a comfortable place."

"Like a chair?"

"Yes, like a chair." Then he bought me a Happy Meal.

With the disappearance of my mother the antics of the dollhouse seemed to be less interesting so I went back to discovering lost civilizations out in the woods behind our house. I looked for Mars in the night sky and tried to imagine the world three thousand years ago. I'd lay very still, under the stars and travel on caravans through ancient worlds.

The next morning we had runny, undercooked, hardboiled eggs for breakfast. Dave stared down at his plate.

"There's a diner down off the highway," I said, trying to be helpful.

"Yeah," he said, standing. Then he threw the plates in the trash.

The glass plates.

After breakfast I went into my room to get my new magic rocks and saw Hank lying face down on the tiled floor. When the coast was clear I sneaked across the hall and put him in my mother's empty dollhouse. There were no porcelain cats, no felt covered birds in tiny cages with no vocal cords, no squatters, no renters, no nothing. Just a big, empty, perfect house that looked good if you were looking in. Hank hated it. There wasn't a drop of booze anywhere.

Dave went outside to smoke a joint. I heard the glass door slide shut. Finally I walked into the kitchen to finish my homework. Dave came in, bleary eyed, looking like someone hit him in the head with a rock.

"You okay?" he asked.

"Yeah." But really I was kind of bored so I was happy when Sadie had a relapse and the Butler drained the bank account.

On Tuesday Dave left me alone in the house. He made me promise not to turn on the stove or tell my grandmother I was ever by myself. I read a Hardy Boys mystery, ate leftover Italian, then padded down the hall, and stared at the empty dollhouse in my mother's room. There was something about its perfection that made it tainted, jaded, unfit.

"I'll drink to that," Sadie said, just before running off to Mexico.

Later that evening Dave guided my mother through the door. Her eyes were heavy, with dark circles underneath.

"Someday," she told me over breakfast the next morning, "you'll get married and have a house, too and you'll be happy you learned something from that dollhouse."

"You're not married," I pointed out.

She stared down into her grape juice. Dave hustled me out of the kitchen and took me to my French lesson.

"I don't want the dollhouse anymore," I announced in the car.

"Cotton, now isn't the time to start changing things around. Just play with the dollhouse the way your mother wants."

"But I don't want it."

"It's just a silly toy," he said, sighing.

"No, it's something else," and I started crying.

The dollhouse loomed dark over my thoughts placed on the floor in-between the dresser and window. Four stories tall, filled to the brim, secrets stashed in every drawer. Late at night, when everyone else was sleeping, it would whisper and creak like it was alive.

So, I started sleeping in the hall again. This time my mother ignored me.

For days I sat at the kitchen table, plotting. How does a seven year old make an entire house just disappear. We had a hammer in the kitchen junk drawer but I knew my mother would blow a gasket over destruction. I slept on it, obsessed, considered my options, begged for aliens to come and take it away, slept on it again, paced the hall in my footed pajamas, obsessed and then at the end of the week the light bulb clicked on so bright, it nearly burst. That night while everyone was sleeping I took the rubber people out to the side of the house and buried them.

"Cotton, where's the family I bought for the house?"

Not bothering to glance up from the Hardy Boy's mystery, I said, "They're not a family and I don't know."

"Well, they were here a few days ago."

"Yes, they were," I picked at the dirt under my fingernails.

"And you don't know what happened to them?"

"Nope. Maybe the dog ate them."

Later that night I eavesdropped outside the bedroom door.

"Don't you think the whole thing is a little creepy and a little odd?" My mother asked Dave.

The Christmas tree was upside down in the trash. It was snowing. Jimmy Carter was on the TV again.

Dave shook his head hopelessly and let it go.

I went back to my room thinking about the rubber people. If Sadie had been there she would have said, "Hank, honey, hasn't anyone noticed that the backside of the house doesn't have a wall? Don't you think that's strange? I mean, people could be watching us."

Angeline would've heard the whole thing while she was dusting the furniture with a cotton ball. Sam would have been wondering why there were so many lamps and no electricity.

And Hank would have stopped making gin martini's long enough to say, "Honey, I think you're making a big deal out of nothing. I mean, we have three sides. So what if the back is missing. It's always been that way."

Tolstoy & the Checkout Girl

Tonya was the only thing that made him smile. The purple and blue streaks in her hair reflected morning sun perfectly. She was the checkout girl at the Sav A Lot. He shuffled through her line in his heavy woolen pants. Tonya snapped and popped her gum. Watermelon. Sour apple. Sweet wild cherry. An intoxicating fragrance to be sure.

Tonya blew a bubble, then asked, "Will that be all?"

Tolstoy dropped his eyes to the cracked floor. "Da."

He glanced up fast enough to see her cock her head to one side, her ponytail slapping her shoulder. She was watermelon today.

"You're going to die of heat exhaustion if you don't ditch that get up."

Tolstoy looked down at his trousers. He'd learn to adjust. To what he wasn't sure. Or for how long.

"$22.36," Tonya popped, pulling her head back in place. Pink and blue glitter sparkled on her eyelids. He wanted to dust his body with those pink and blue flecks. He pulled money from his pocket, handing it to Tonya to count. American currency made no sense. He counted in Rubles.

Her fingernails were bright orange, tips painted white. She counted his money, handed back change and whispered, "Be careful out there. The world is mean to freaks." Then she turned to the person behind him in line and asked, "Did you find everything you need today?"

I found you, Tolstoy thought. He stepped through the strange sliding doors into a wall of heat that consumed the rest of his thoughts.

Until he flopped down on the cool, tile floor under the humming contraption that blew cold air day and night. He peeled off layers of clothes one by one, like an onion, it made him cry.

In the evening he awoke to the whoosh of America, this strange land. Horns, people bustling about on the sidewalk below his room. Down the hall a man sang horribly off key.

Tolstoy rose from the cool floor and picked up the map the police had given him when they found him in the bus station. He smoothed the map across the empty table. A star marked the city of Delray Beach, Florida. From there his finger trailed over the world, across the Atlantic, through Europe, up to Russia where it stopped and tapped Moscow, before sliding south to his hometown. Such a long way to travel with no recollection. He was so young, yet remembered being an old man, like time fleeting backwards.

Tolstoy stared at the blank, plaster walls. He stood up and found a pen in a drawer. With precision he wrote a single word on the white wall. Astapovo. He stepped back and read the word over and over until he began to repeat it aloud. When a creamy orange sunset glowed in his windows he pulled a can of sardines out of his grocery bag and arranged the little fishes on crackers. They stared up at him. Rays of sunlight stretched low across the horizon in pink golds. He looked at the surface of the lake. Blades of grass jutted from the shore. Wind. Sky. Grass. All so different from where he'd come from. He was so displaced he couldn't remember why he'd left. How he'd gotten here.

He pulled a thick bag of kopeks from his pocket, wondering what they could buy. They were so old and big. He turned one over in his hand, deciding to give it to Tonya as a gift. Tonya of the green eyes, blue smock, bare arms, rings on every finger, even her thumb, especially her thumb where a silver genie wrapped around her finger staring down into a crystal ball. He wanted to touch her hand, lay his finger on the tiny crystal ball and gaze at their future together. He sat down on the small sofa and conjured images of fields rolling past, across Russian summers.

In the morning he woke to the sound of geese, made coffee and set out in the blazing sun to buy ice cream. The heat was everywhere. Like the cold in Russia. A life spent in extremes. At 7:32 AM the electric doors of the Sav A Lot swooshed open. The cool air enveloped him. The smell of all things unfamiliar brought a smile to his face. There was no explaining this America.

In the checkout line he asked Tonya what she was doing.
"What do you mean?"
"Here. You are always here. Why?"
"Because I work here. Don't you have a job?"
He looked down at his worn boots. "No."
"Well I am here every day from 7-3PM slaving my ass off to go to Cosmetology School."
"Where you study the cosmos?"
"Makeup and hair, baby."
He was relieved to be the only one standing in line. A crowd of old men clustered together at a checkout near the door. Tonya was close to the thing she called video rental, out of sight, a precious moment.
"Well," she popped her sour apple gum, so green it glowed, "like beauty school, you know?"
Like the places his sisters and aunts had gone when he was little. To have their hair made pretty and fingernails glazed cherry red.

"Cause I think I'd be real good at it. What do you think?"

He nodded. "Da."

She eyed his unkempt beard, his hair growing down past his shoulders.

"I could practice on you."

He needed help. This America seemed so much more modern than his Russia. He'd been on his morning walk, watching the birds in the sky. He'd sat down in the train station to rest, because it was cold and because he'd been up so late writing.

Then he'd woken up here.

One long dream. He imagined.

Except the heat made it real.

Still it must be a dream.

Never before had he seen stores with row upon row of food stacked to the ceiling. Lamps glowed, all night.

Electricity, his lord of the land said.

This electricity surged in his mind alongside Tonya.

Who was snapping her fingers in his face. "Are you alright?"

Tolstoy blinked, "Da."

"Well you look like you left your body."

To illustrate how all right he was he backed away from the checkout counter and fell over sideways.

The woman in line behind him dropped her broccoli and screamed.

Tonya ran around the counter. "Someone get the manager. We've got a customer down."

The manager had a mustache that bobbed up and down on his top lip like a hairy, fat caterpillar. He wrapped his arm gently around Tolstoy's shoulder and led him to a small, square room with a concrete floor. The plain room made him yearn for the gilded light fixtures of home, the silk wall coverings, the sounds of his sister playing violin.

At a metal table he sat.

The manager opened a can of soda. "Drink this. It could be your blood sugar. My wife faints all of the time." Then, "And take off that god awfully hot shirt."

Tolstoy unbuttoned his favorite shirt. The charcoal gray wool with silver buttons. The one Oleg made for him. His white chest glowed beneath the buzzing lights. Dark patches of hair like furry islands.

The manager opened a locker from a row against the far wall and pulled out a shirt that looked like the one Tonya wore but bigger and handed it to him. The fabric was cheap, scratchy but felt cool against his skin. He was grateful. The manager put coins in a machine and another soda can tumbled to the bottom. He handed it to Tolstoy, told him to wait, sit quietly, he'd come back later.

He was drinking his soda, watching the clock on the wall above a shelf full of items he had no names for when Tonya walked in. His English, while sufficient in many ways was not as good as his French or Russian. Although he'd been having trouble remembering both lately. It could be the heat or dementia. Both were beyond his control at the moment.

Tonya set a bag on the table. "I bought us food to make lunch. I'm going to take you back to my place and keep an eye on you. You're always buying cookies and ice cream and wearing enough clothes to get you through an Artic winter. No wonder you passed out."

"Okay," he said.

"Okay, what?"

"You can take me."

Cool air blew on his face from the little openings in Tonya's strange mobile auto that rolled on wheels with no horse to pull. He closed his eyes. Tonya of the sweet wild cherry.

"Listen," she said, looking over at him. "I'll take you back to my place. You're still really pale. If you don't get your color back, Wayne said to take you to the ER. I don't think you should be alone."

No, not ever again, he thought. Not since I found you. Like gypsies we will cross the Siberian plains in Summer.

A small apartment with a concrete patio was home. He watched her toss her keys and purse on a table.

"We'll start lunch, then play beauty parlor."

He was hungry. Still a little dizzy. In the small kitchen she set the food on a table and handed him a bag of potatoes and a knife. "Peel these," she instructed.

Tolstoy pulled a dusty, brown skinned potato from the bag. The weight of it in his palm jerked him back to childhood. The potato endured the long, harsh Russian winter. The potato and man. The solid brown skinned, thick vegetable sustained winter after winter in the dark, heavy nights of his boyhood. Now, here he was with the weight of his past in his palm and the dazzling brightness of his future. There were no wells in this place, no buckets. Just a pipe where water ran smooth into a sink, over his hands, cool.

As the potatoes boiled on the stove, Tonya tilted his head forward into the sink. One of her hands pressed lightly into his back, the other on his neck. He wanted to shrink to the size of her hand so that she could hold every inch of him. The water was loud and hot and relaxing. She shampooed his hair. The scent of fresh blossoms exploded in the warm, rising air. She massaged his scalp and a deep longing crept into him. He wanted to fall asleep with the feeling of her massaging his temples. He felt a deep urge to know her, possess her. The water rushed past his ears, lulling him into a sense of isolation but he was not fooled. She was right there.

She rinsed, wrapped a towel around his head, led him into the living room, where she motioned to a chair. On the table a case was open. Metal scissors, devices he had no names for. She bit her bottom lip, tilting his chin this way and that, staring at his hair, his beard.

So close she was. Close enough to see the fine hairs of her eyebrows, the freckles on her chest into the curve of her breast, the shape of her eyes outlined in dark blue makeup, the amber flecks in her green eyes. The way her bare shoulders looked like rising moons falling. He imagined himself as a gyroscope, spinning in the palm of her hand.

"Okay, you're pretty scraggily." She stepped back. "I'm going to cut your hair, then your beard, then I'll give you a nice shave. Any objections?"

Tolstoy shook his head. Oleg was in charge of such things back home. Oleg who pressed his clothes and packed his trunks and trimmed his hair. Oleg who brought him breakfast and picked up his letters from the post. Oleg who must have arranged this trip.

Then for a long time the only sound was the snip snip snip of the scissors trimming away the parts of him that had grown wild.

Tonya's fingers brushed against his cheek. So much of him was falling to the floor. He thought she'd snip and snip until he disappeared. Until all of the pieces of him were on the floor. Until he fell to pieces because her hand against his skin brought an unbearable tremble. She was still wearing her nametag. The one that spelled her name and had a heart drawn on the side. He thought of the potato. If he could just explain to her the absolute silence of a long, winter night. If he could explain how by Spring you knew everyone's mood by the sound of their footsteps. How the cold claimed everything on the other side of the window so you warmed your fingers on a candle and wrote passages deep into the night.

He pointed to candle on the table. "Would you light it?"

"Are you trying to set the mood?"

He looked down at the floor, pieces of him scattered.

She whacked him softly on the shoulder, "I'm just kidding."

And he thought, you are not a kid but said nothing. The light danced wildly next to Tonya as she cut his hair. It would grow back. Time would pass. He knew these things.

Her skin was a soft, peach glow. Shadows flickered. All of his life he'd known these flickering images. He'd imagined they were his mother and father watching over him. Friendly ghosts. Friendly, featureless, paper cut outs of a child.

The shadows of her fingers snip snip snipped against the walls. Then came the hot towels. The utter bliss of hot towels, fingers against his temples again. The pressure that massaged away how he'd stumbled through this part of his life, the one so unfamiliar it had no name. Her bracelets clanked softly next to his ear. He listened. Her big emerald green eyes watched. He heard the swish of the blade in water, the familiar tap tap.

Then Tonya pulled the blade at a careful angle against his cheek and the mask that concealed him was stripped away.

"So do you always sport this big, hairy look?"

He could not remember. "I do not know."

"So where are you from?" she asked.

"A town south of Moscow."

She readjusted his head gently. "Hold still," she said and he did. Then, "God, what's it like over there. The farthest I've ever been was summers on Long Island."

Tolstoy blinked.

"So, what brings you to sunny Florida?"

"I'm not sure."

"What do you mean?"

He shrugged.

She readjusted him. "Like you can't remember? Like amnesia?"

"Da."

"That is freaking cool," she said, excited and snip snip snipped faster. "Did you hit your head or something? What's the last thing you remember?"

"I remember being on my morning walk, looking down at the tiny ants, wondering if I was too tall for this world."

"Interesting," she said.

The swish swish swish and the tap tap tap.

Within minutes he felt the cool air on his face and cheeks, unburdened. The beauty of a moment alone with a woman, clear and light, like the fields of his childhood where he ran. Fields of tall grass, trailing open hands across the soft tips. The warmth of late spring meeting summer, the thaw, gently sweet, a rolling creek. Tatiana's hand in his. Pulling him forward. Come, Tatiana yelled, come.

"Shit," Tonya said.

He turned. "What?"

She set the bowl of hot towels down. "I forgot to clock out. Crap. It drives Wayne crazy when I do that and screws up his payroll." She looked at the clock. "I have to run down and clock out. I'll be right back."

The door slammed behind her. The flames sputtered.

He stood and walked to the kitchen. In the fading, summer light insects hummed and chirped in a loud buzz outside. The frozen land of his past held no such songs. Here the earth and sky merged into a wash of apricot and pink. Tangerines on the counter ripened, the air fragrant. He laid his hands on the sink of this unfamiliar world and looked out the window where a reflection greeted him. A tall, darkly handsome man with a strong jaw and broad shoulders. The kind of man he would tip his hat to at a party. The light shimmered and he imagined a place like this in the world for himself. When Tonya returned he'd take her hand and beg her to become a gypsy with him, to toss the blue and purple streaks of her hair into the wind and ride. With him. Across a tundra glowing with moist, warm light. A bracelet sat on the counter. The kind with charms and feathers. He picked it up. Very slowly he closed his eyes, squeezing it tight.

The train station at Astapovo was quiet, nearly deserted. Tolstoy opened his eyes. Rows upon rows of empty benches unfolded before him. He looked down at his hands, limp in his lap. Then to his feet propped on his old trunk. His old, black boots were scuffed, the toes and heels like smooth stones emerging from darkness. Now he understood. He'd fallen asleep, drifted away. So weary. His hands were wrinkled, deep lines written in his skin by the years of life. He longed for the smooth hands that touched Tonya's face. So old he was upon waking from his dream. A dream of the future. A dream, nevertheless. Never one to sigh, he allowed the exhalation of breath. How old was he? Seventy? Eighty? Ninety? He couldn't remember anymore. A deep silence enveloped him. He'd told no one it was his time to go but Oleg must have known. Winter bristled through the cracks. A chill rushed past his face but he was warm. Tonya with the purple and blue streaks in her hair, the wild watermelon breath. Tonya. He'd known her once. Somewhere. In a dream.

Yet, so real. More real than right now which dimmed more every second, graying around the edges so that the rows of empty benches receded, disappearing into nothingness. The whistle of the last train rolled into the distance. His eyelids were heavy, pulled to another dream. Green fields of spring. He wondered what would become of the Serfs without him, Oleg, and the others. A roar of butterfly wings rushed in and he listened, feeling the lift as the sound of laughter returned to take him home.

The Descent

The prince who awakened me from my slumber was not my husband.

"Marla?"

Samuel is sitting on the sofa reading The Times. "Penny for your thoughts."

I point to my day planner. I'll give you a nickel if you just go away.

"Oh," his eyes say, dropping back to the page.

Need, Want & Desire play a game in my head. I follow them out to a dark labyrinth where they talk gibberish and take shape. The fire sings a song. They take my hands, laying them against my own skin and they chant, rattle, shake, across dark skies with no moonlight. They part my legs and plead. I obey. They dance into ferocious cries of pleasure.

Everything happens in reel time now. I am starring in the French Film that is my life. Sometimes it is black and white with no sound. I turn the volume up. When I open my eyes, my lover is watching me. He says, "I had to get up in the middle of the night to get a blanket because you had the sheet wrapped around you."

"Why didn't you wake me?"

"Because you look so good in it."

We are making the film of us. The unrated version. You get the picture.

My bathroom mirror has become my psychologist. I don't understand, I am whining to my other self. I am confused. I am driven to live my life at the expense of destroying another. Driven. I hear Larry Adler backing his car out of his driveway next door. He is tall, blonde, dazzling and doesn't cheat on his wife. "Not me," I say, confidently looking the psychologist in the eye, applying gloss to my cheating lips. "I am having an affair." I hate myself for being so flip about it but today at 3PM I am having a board meeting in room 504 of the Waterford Inn. *Naked.*

The curtains are pulled so tight that I can only see an outline of my lover's face. "I have to be back before dinner," I say, rolling over, biting into his neck. His hands ride up to my hips. I am scaling the tower walls. We begin making sense.

Out in the cool, evening air he wraps his arms around me. The French film that is us drifts off around the corner. Then we cut.

We're having defensive behavior for dinner again.
"I've seen you for two hours all week," Samuel says, squeezing his wine glass, laying blame. "I wish you'd never taken that job, Marla."

I think I am an incomplete human being cloned from an earlier version of myself that was damaged. I want to think I'm on the verge of a breakthrough but what I'm really doing is cheating on my husband. I'm not stupid. I do it every day, habitually, like a chain smoker, sneaking out back, or upstairs, or to the broom closet for my fix. I want to travel across the distance of my lover's chest, and ride a caravan down to his lips where his tongue waits like an oasis.

At a dinner party a few days later Samuel is droning on. "Charles was listening to Chet Baker the other night and he hummed every note in a perfect pitch,"
"That's our Charles," I chime in.

Clarice unfolds herself from the sofa, wobbling on martini legs. "Yes, it goes without saying," she says, dismissively.

Samuel reaches out a hand to steady her as she passes. In a fit of irreverence she waves her cherry lacquered nails, "So what. I know all of the words to Amazing Grace. Nobody ever makes that the topic of conversation."

Charles is in the kitchen pouring a fresh one when I walk in with the empty tray. I set it on the counter and he turns with that wayward smile that captivates people.

"Can I ask you a question?" I ask.

"You just did."

"Then, can I ask another?"

"Fire away."

"Have you ever cheated on Clarice?"

"That's a loaded question."

"Not as loaded as you."

"Hmmm," he wonders aloud, raising his glass in a toast. "Why on earth would you ask such a thing? Have you been following me?"

On Wednesday I am in my perfect house, with its perfect smell, and it's perfectly placed furniture and I begin to cry. The sensation is overwhelming, crushing, like the news of death knocking the wind out of me. I have been jerked from my current fantasy back to the original reality I don't want anymore. My knees begin to crumble. It is dark. The Grandfather clock chimes. I will do anything not to feel the way I felt before. The phone is ringing. I answer it because I am trained to be polite.

"Hi," Larry Adler is saying, so chipper. "Hey, Judy and I were wondering..."

Blah...Blah...Blah...Judy and I were wondering why we don't ever seem to be as simultaneously miserable and ecstatic as you. We've hired a landscaper and boy has he done wonders for our marriage...Uh, I mean, lawn. Ha-Ha. Samuel looked a little blue the other day so we bought him a wine roasted chicken. You must have been off at that new job of yours. He feels better now. We all feel better. Ah, chicken...

"Marla?"

"Yes."

"Can we borrow the hedge trimmer?"

In the moments between then and now I learn that the imperfections of my life form a perfect puzzle.

The tile in my hallway is jade green. The color of envy. I set my shopping bags down, turning on the lamp. The messages play one by one. Message deleted...next message. The sound of Evan's voice echoes in my head. Like a sniper, my eyes scan all directions looking for my husband. "I am sitting on the floor in the ER," Evan is saying. But he's not really saying it because this is a recording . It is reel time. Words catch in the back of my throat. I hear his tears slap against his cheeks, burning. Somehow I kneel, letting his slow cry ring in my ears. I am stunned into a silence that hums inside my head joining me forever with him in tragedy.

The words 'heart attack' and 'father' leap out through the sobs. 'Dead' comes later. But this is just make believe and we are just a fantasy and real things like this don't happen to people who are living in French films without any sound. Desperate to live out this moment I rewind and replay the message seventeen times before I stop counting. I don't know what to say. I want to be there, out beyond flesh and memory in that final thread weaving itself into the fabric of circumstance.

In the middle of this inexcusable, habit forming addiction that forms a craving in the pit of my stomach I am touched. I am touched because I am the called and not the caller. I am the needed and not the needy. I am whole and smart and wise. I have abandoned a marriage of matching towels and suicidal howls of boredom to descend into the body of another for a fraction of infinity.

This is reel time.

The stop light is red. Samuel's fingertips dance over the steering wheel. I glance over at him. Then I really look. This time I am looking at the angles of his face, the well defined cheekbones, nose, eyelashes the color of bleached wood, the flecks of green and gray in his eyes, the seductive way his eyelids lay languidly amid his face. I am chronicling in some way the beauty of all that he is and all that he is not. I need to freeze it into my mind's eye so that I can take it out on long train rides away from him.

"I have to go away on business for a few days." I say, replaying the phone message over and over in my mind.

His jaw tightens. "Where?"

"Utah. A conference for work."

"Really?"

I close my eyes and nod, unable to utter another lie in such a confined space.

"Oh, god, Marla. Strangers at work trying to make eye contact is so much better than some woman standing in line at the grocery store bitching at you because you're taking too long to write a check." Clarice throws her legs on the table like a cowboy after a long day.

I tell her about Evan because I have to tell someone. I tell her because I must. In order to make it real I must make it known so I tread out in shark filled waters. But I don't tell her everything. I tell her he's a stranger at work who flirts with me but Evan isn't a stranger anymore. For instance, I know the scars on his chest are from a motorcycle accident in England. Memory is liquid. *Listen.* I tell her more.

Clarice stares at the ashes floating to the tabletop, looking for the shape to form a message.

I let my face fall into my hands trying to stop this feeling that I have to escape or destroy another to become whole. Clarice taps me with her toe. I float out into the green of her eyes.

"Marla, it's okay. Change only comes to you when you're changing." Her smile is so broad and beautiful that for a moment I am completely stumped.

Tears fill my eyes. "I don't know what it means..."

"Sure you do. Think about it, Marla. You're on the verge of an answer. That's a powerful place to be."

I am ascending the staircase of my childhood home. The stairs creak. The plaster ripples. Something comes into focus. I walk to the very top, up and out onto the roof. I am on top of the tallest building in the world. I jump. I am falling, falling, falling ... When I wake in the hotel room in Salt Lake City, Evan is holding me tight. I watch his chest rise and fall until I drift back into dreams.

Charles is drunk again. And clever. He rouses a spirited hand in the air, musing, "Zen koan for the day: If one grain of rice cries, does it cause the others around it to expand?"

Clarice is on the other side of the doorway and I hear her mumble, "Asshole..."

I step into the kitchen to make a pot of coffee. I ask her if they're having marital problems.

"What?" she asks, astonished. "Are you telling me that I'm married to that *asshole*?"

Reel time. Friday afternoon. Two shots of espresso. Three cups of coffee and a pack of cigarettes. I am ready to take over a small third world country. Evan opens the hotel door, naked, scotch and soda. Sex on too much caffeine is like riding on an out of control Ferris wheel. Tense, grinding, now, numbness. I cannot fly. I cannot soar. I cannot let go of the last stupid thought I had. We are facing the wall, doing primal things, growling, tempting. The rhythm is hypnotic, everywhere, all over, in front of us. Snippets of earlier conversations flash across the screen of my mind. *If you want to work for the most corrupt institution ever, then work for the military... I'm too generous, too naïve... My first wife... I'm a Virgo with a Scorpio rising but I don't know what that means... I moved from Kansas...then my girlfriend left me...God, all I wanted was a cup of coffee and I was stuck in line for over an hour...*
I cannot focus. There are only pieces. I am dizzy with the pieces. I should leave. I do not feel good about this part. My brain is the autobahn.

I begin to think that cars are like thoughts. We create them and drive them obsessively over and over. Then we trade them in for what someone from an advertising agency tells us we should want. Factory rebates. Too much caffeine. What everyone else wants. It's all the same thing.

"What do you want?" Evan says, logging out of the system.
"I need those reports."
For the first time he swirls around in his chair and we make eye contact. I am not thinking I will leave my husband. I am not thinking anything when I close the door. I am carefully watching his starched white shirt rise and fall with his breath, the top of his tie pulled away from his neck, the way his suspenders lay against his chest.

Lifting a file from a plastic tray, he says, "I'm one step ahead of you. I finished the reports. Why don't you come have a drink with me?"

3:19 PM. I am supposed to be sending a quarterly sales report but instead I am pricing edible body paint online.

It is the feeling of the heat and not knowing where his mouth will land that is so disorienting. Words travel across great distances to hold me. The sounds beyond the hotel window are like the blood swishing in my veins. These moments twist and surrender to a thin blade of light looking to feast on anything. *Like this*, I keep telling myself. Then I am racing to catch up again. I am whispering words I have never heard before and they bubble out into the air where he sucks them into his mouth, repeating them back to me word for word. My clothes fall from my body like drops of rain.

We are all god's children making that voyage down into a descent of our own design.

Clarice's eyes dart around the housekeeper like an animal at the zoo that's been taken from the wild, forced into captivity. "I've been volunteering at a homeless shelter." She crosses her legs, then uncrosses.

"It's probably good for you," I say, because maybe it is.

"That's what everyone says." Then she pours a drink at 11AM, distracted. "God, Marla, I just— Charles stays up all night pacing, staring at those damn windows. When he finally comes to bed, he dreams and dreams, tossing and turning. It's like sleeping with an angry beast. His dreams give me nightmares."

Chills run up my spine.

Dark circles swell like a current under her eyes. "Charles has always been listless," she says. Smoke spirals into the air. "It's like he's killing off parts of himself he no longer wants. I watch the parts die, starved, abandoned and it drives me to the edge."

On Tuesday I enter to find Clarice's body slackened over the toilet, vomiting blood. The kitchen has flooded because of a faulty pipe. Candles have melted down all over the floor. We hold hands, praying, singing old church hymnals the nuns taught us in school until Charles finally gets there. Two hours late. Stinking of gin.

"I didn't expect him to be so attractive," Evan says, pumping gas.

"Who?" I ask, digging through my purse for change.

"Samuel."

A gunshot rings out in my mind, blasting every thought into outer space. I am watching my reflection in the window, "What did you say?"

"I mean, he's not just attractive, he's incredibly handsome."

"Where did you see my husband?" I sputter.

"I was introduced to him at a cocktail party last night. I shook his hand with the same hand I use to take your panties off." He leans against the car as the gas pumps. "I didn't know he was English. He sounded like Jude Law. Proper. I kind of liked him." He turns, leaning over the hood of the car, trailing a finger out to meet me. "I had to like him. He has what I want."

"You went to a party without me?"

"I drove over to The Regis to book our room for tonight. A friend of mine was having a party in the lounge. He talked me into one drink. I'm glad I went. It's nice to meet the competition."

"You don't have any competition."

He raises an eyebrow. "None?"

"The minute I looked across that room and saw you there was only you."

"Even if being with me is complicated?"

"Being with you is easy. Everything else is complicated."

We profess our love in parking lots in-between yellow lines. We tell secrets streetlamps overhear. Housekeeping attendants become the kindly mothers we never had.

When the call comes at 3 AM Samuel is the one who answers. I roll over, horrified it might be Evan. Samuel turns on the light, reaches for his jeans, says, "Yes...yes...I know the place," and then hangs up.

My heart is still, my blood is placid, floating. I feel faint. "Who was that?" I manage.

Samuel stands, naked, pulling his jeans up from his ankles. I look at him in his nudity, his vulnerability, his manliness. He looks out over me like a shadow, grinding his teeth.

"Samuel," I say, sitting up, exposed.

His eyes travel the distance of my body softly, evenly, stopping on my face. For a moment he is my husband and I am his wife. Then he says, "Clarice stole a baby from a woman at the homeless shelter."

Sometimes when I am all alone I sit at my desk and pretend that the world is ending. People are dying outside my windowless office. I do not hear them. They die quietly because there is no more air for them. I do not know them. I sit in my office with my artificial air and I breathe. Gripping my hair tight in my hands, I pray and plead and beg myself to go back to my husband. I bribe myself. I tell myself that for the rest of my life I can have anything I want. Then I look up and Evan is standing in the doorway, smiling, asking me if I'd like to go to Rome.

Charles is beside himself, pacing, swearing, smoking in the police station even though he's been told by a fat cop to stop about a hundred times. I sit on a wooden bench not made to be sat on while Samuel works out the details at the desk. Charles stops, pulls his fingertips together, looks to be on the verge of some philosophical revelation then stops, grinds his teeth and growls, "Damn you, Clarice."

When a woman emerges from a side office I realize that it must be her. She has been crying and doesn't look homeless but is wearing old clothes, a faded poofy jacket from the late 70's with a matted faux fur collar. Samuel is the first to make eye contact with her and something close to a smile weaves itself across her face. I look in my purse for lip gloss, eyeliner, anything to avoid looking at her. But I do look, slyly, the way a con man watches a pool game. Charles stares at her like she's from another planet. It's embarrassing.

Clarice is in a room with no mirrors, dainty, removed, oblivious. "We were going for ice cream," she says so cheerfully that it forms tears in my eyes.

"You were at the fucking airport," Charles screams.

Samuel squeezes my hand as if to say, at least we don't have these kinds of problems.

"So what? Maybe I was." Clarice swings her legs around, standing up, ready to leave. "Fuck you, Charles."

I am dreaming again. I walk to the very top, up and out onto the roof. I am on top of the tallest building in the world. I jump. I am falling, falling, falling...

Samuel is snoring, wheezing really. My jerking awake doesn't startle him. I don't know what to do because a few seconds before I jumped from the tallest building in the world so I go to the musty basement and watch reruns of Wheel of Fortune until I collapse on a cot. Samuel finds me the next morning. The starch on his shirt is shiny. I get up to go to work.

"It's Saturday," he says.

"So it is," I say, glancing at the digital face of my cell phone.

"I thought maybe we could have brunch."

"Brunch. *Really?* And maybe some dessert."

"I don't know why you're so hostile. I'm your husband. It is natural for me to find you desirable."

"Desirable," I snort.

Clarice's attire consists of flannel pajamas with pink bunny rabbits chasing each other and fuzzy slippers. She won't look at me because she's too busy painting her fingernails with liquid paper while a very large orderly stands to the side watching like a hawk. She is thinner, frail, more beautiful if such a thing can be true.

"Clarice," I whisper, leaning across the metal table.

Her green eyes drift to the tall windows covered in bars. I touch her hand.

"Clarice," I say, so quietly I can barely hear myself, "I'm having an affair."

A wistful smile curls over her face in waves, delightful waves of ecstasy, and she claps her hands together in such a joyous way that for a moment I forget her court ordered psychiatric care for stealing babies her own body denies her. The angels come to us, flapping their wings against our cheeks until we are drunk with delight.

"Really?" she says, clasping my hand and I know my best friend is back. "The one from work? The one with scars on his chest?"

"Yes," I nod, pinching my excitement into a tiny whisper.

"Do you have a picture of him?"

"No, I don't keep anything around...No, wait. I do." Digging through my purse I find a company photo of several people, Evan is in the background to the left.

"Oh God," pulling her hand to her mouth, "does he take off your panties and make you scream his name and give you diamonds and champagne?"

"Yeah," I say, thinking about the answer, exhaling, looking for the truth.

The nurse on duty wheels a cart over, dispensing meds.

"God, Marla, I'm so happy for you," Clarice says, swallowing the rest of her afternoon away in a little white pill.

Reel time.

"Evan?"

"Yes?"

"Can we go away?"

He rolls over so fast in bed there is wind against my cheeks. "Are you serious?"

"Yes."

"For how long?"

"Forever."

I am so taken by what I've just said that I cannot swallow or move. I am suspended out in wild time where life changing decisions are made. In the dark I can see his face, so touching, so elegant, barely breathing, reaching into his carrying case for something. I am so naked I am nude, completely revealed.

He slowly slides a ring onto my finger. Neither of us says anything. We just know. For the first time in my life I am not just making love, I am making sense.

From sun up til sun down we swim in a shot of vodka. The man who feels everything and the woman that felt nothing. People call it love.

On a very normal Thursday afternoon Evan drives us over to my well manicured neighborhood to tell my husband that I am leaving. It's the way it should be. A passing of the torch. Man to man and all of that shit. Samuel thinks about hitting him. I can see it in his eyes but in the end he steps aside, instructing, "Her stuff is in the bathroom, in the bedroom. You'll know what's hers. Take whatever you like."

Watching all of this from the car at the curb feels like reel time. It occurs to me that I may never have silk wallpaper or a pool house but now I have Rome. I step out and lean against the car wearing my big Audrey Hepburn sunglasses and I smoke a long cigarette. Samuel is watching me from the window in his study. I blow smoke in rings but really I'm telling him to go blow something else.

Clarice does a striptease in the lounge to celebrate and the orderlies put a straitjacket on her, dragging her kicking and screaming down the hall. This is the first time Evan has ever met my best friend.

Before they have a chance to stick her with the shut up serum she yells, "Screw the revolution. I want a man who makes me sing."

She may be crazy, but she's right.

Evan's lips press against mine in the parking lot. Now our secret is something else. Now our secret is safe.

Charles calls my cell phone just before Evan and I board the plane.

"I thought you knew I was cheating on Clarice. That night in the kitchen. You restless little devil. Samuel is very angry. I think he needs a psychiatrist..."

That's funny, don't we all.

The boarding gates are empty. Fluorescent lights buzz. There is beauty everywhere.

That night, on the plane, I jump in my dreams and I am falling, falling, falling and an angel with iridescent wings floats up to me and whispers, "Why don't you use the stairs?"

When I wake, we are hovering twenty thousand feet above the Italian skyline. I am starring in the French film that is my life. Primal, restless, hungry. The unrated version. You get the picture. Static crackles. The Captain's voice comes over the loudspeaker, "Please fasten your seat belts. We are beginning our descent."

I feel like I should scream, howl, but I look around and see that everyone is sleeping. My blood is wine. I am reel.

The Temp

At Bradley Biomedical a Hungarian man named Nicola worked three offices down from mine. He'd come to my desk and give me notes and corrections and I'd plan our entire future in sixty second intervals as he stood at my desk. Stacks of French Literature would cover our floors. We'd smoke Dunhill cigarettes in the evening and drink bottles of red wine.

"Do you have those corrections, June?" His accent was rich, like thick cigar smoke.

"Huh?"

He raised his eyebrow, which made his mouth tighten, ready for a kiss. "The corrections to the Hamburg Medical Group letters of agreement?"

Letters. Love letters. I sighed, handing over a folder. "Yes, I typed up the copies and the new correspondence for you."

He leaned across my desk and touched my nose with the tip of his finger. His perfect finger that I longed to touch with my tongue. "Oh, June, how much nicer my life is with you looking out for me."

The phone rang, interrupting. I wanted to shred it. I smiled quickly and answered. After a second, I said, "It's for you. Again. What's with all of the phone calls?"

"Bureaucrats," he said grimly.

I watched him walk away. We'd eat ripe cherries and I'd lay with my head in his lap at night and I'd read *Lolita* aloud. I'd say her name Lo Lee Ta and let the Ta tap on my tongue. We'd buy an old record player and listen to Chet Baker and Nina Simone albums. Old, scratchy tunes that kept us up late and made me want to crawl onto his lap naked. In public we'd whisper naughty bits in each other's ears and live in apartment above a bakery owned by a woman named Gertrude who baked strudel. We'd talk about fascist foreign policy designed to usher in Imperialist ideals and our favorite Japanese poems from the twelfth century. We'd light candles and in-between our words there would be the silence of two people always listening for what the other wasn't saying but feeling...

"June?"

I looked up. My Supervisor was chewing on the end of her pen. I'd been on her shit list ever since my first day when she'd announced to me that she looked very young for her age. "How old do you think I am?" she'd asked cheerfully, that fateful day.

Like a sucker, I'd answered truthfully. "42."

Correct age. Wrong answer.

Her smiled disappeared and did not return. *Ever*.

"June, did you type those docs going to Medical Trust?"

I handed her the folder. Go away, Mrs. Easily Offended By People Who Guess Your Real Age.

"Thanks," she said, without a hint of sincerity and walked off.

Where was I? Oh, yes. We'd make pots of Turkish coffee and talk about ancient civilizations and Anna Karenina. A fine layer of dust would settle on our books and tables because we'd keep the windows open to hear the city below and we'd never, ever clean. Like, never, ever. We'd go to art openings and talk about Sartre, Beauvoir, and Camus. He'd wear Hugo Boss and all of our matching luggage would be leather.

"June?"

I looked up.

It was him. Mr. Hot Hungarian.

"Ripe cherries, Anna Karenina and a fine layer of dust? What kind of list are you making, June?"

My cheeks flushed hot and I covered my list with my hand.

"It's just something I'm writing. A story."

"About who?"

About us, I thought. Instead of professing my crush, I said, "Two people in love."

"Two people in love would have dust on their tables. A clean house is the sign of an unhappy marriage," he said.

Married. My heart thumped and flittered.

He tapped my desk contemplatively. "Goodnight, June."

Goodnight, gorgeous.

I glanced across the office. A dark, winter evening bristled outside the windows.

"Take a message if anyone calls and leave it on my desk," he said, hanging around, clutching his briefcase.

"Yes." I nodded, willing him to see how I longed to pop open a bottle of vino and show him my new polka dotted demi bra from the Victoria's Secret Semi-Annual Sale.

He sighed, watching me, then tapped my desk again and walked to the door.

We'd eat fresh figs and toast and take cruises up and down the Danube.

It was Friday night. Snow fluttered from the sky as I walked to my Oldsmobile. I stopped by the bagel shoppe on the way home and bought dinner. Lox and cream cheese on a Rosemary bagel. My roommate was on the phone fighting with his girlfriend. They were mad because he lived in Wisconsin and she lived in Nebraska. It was the same fight they'd been having for a year. Since she left. His Lean Cuisine was burning in the microwave. I went to my room dreaming about Goulash and smoked paprika.

On Monday morning my phone rang at 6:45 AM. Cheryl from Temp to Temp Agency said, "I've got an assignment for you."

"Huh? I'm at Bradley BioMedical."

"That ended Friday."

"What?" I sat up straight.

"Remember?"

"No."

"Well, get a pen. I've got a new assignment."

I didn't want a new assignment. I wanted midnight in Budapest, sitting on his lap, removing his tie with Nina Simone crooning in the background.

"Ready?"

I sighed obnoxiously. "Yes."

My new assignment was across town in East Madison. It took forty-five minutes to get there and forty-five on the return trip which would normally be a perfectly useless piece of information except it meant that by the time I left one job the building that housed my Hungarian was closed.

Finally, after two days of needling my Supervisor to leave early, I did something I'd never done. I left my assignment. I picked up my new Vera Wang ruffled crimson purse and logged out of my computer. Presumably for the last time. I drove straight to Bradley Bio Medical.

My Hungarian's office was empty. I waved down the mail girl pushing her cart at the other end of the hall.

"Is he in a meeting?" I called out to her.

"No. He's gone."

"Where?"

She shrugged. "Hungary. He was here on a temporary visa."

I stood, stunned, my hand on his door, touching the cool, smooth wood. I sighed. What a bunch of suck. In the parking lot I adjusted my rearview mirror. My skin was dry. I reached down to start my Oldsmobile. Cheryl was going to be pissed.

The next few days lumbered along. It was the weekend and I listened to my roommate argue on the phone with his girlfriend while I baked terrible cookies and took bubble baths. On Sunday he asked me to take him to the airport. Finally, a truce had been declared. He was going to Nebraska for a visit. He was honest. If it worked out, he might stay. Great, I shrugged. No job, no boyfriend, no roommate. Everything happens in threes. We loaded up the Oldsmobile with his army issue duffel bags and drove to the airport.

The coffee shop across the street from the airport was what I needed. I dropped my roommate off at departures, wished him good luck and then drove across the street. I was about to step out of my car when Nic walked out the front door holding a cup of coffee.

I hurled myself against my door, tumbling out, yelling, "Nic."

He jumped, turned around disoriented, then laughed. "Oh, June. It is you. I've missed you. They told me you were gone."

"They told me the same thing about you."

His eyes drifted left, then right, the way he did when faced with an interesting point. "Yes. The bureaucrats got me. They won't renew my work visa. It is almost embarrassing."

Not as embarrassing as what I'm about to do. "You know those lists I make, Nic?"

He cocked his head to one side. "The Anna Karenina and fresh ripe cherry lists? What about them, June?"

"I want us to smoke Dunhills at night after a bottle of wine. I will lay with my head in your lap and read Lolita aloud. We'll float on the Danube, eat cherries and strudel and listen to Chet Baker."

"Will we make love while a fine layer of dust covers everything in our apartment?"

My knees actually trembled.

"You are a very beautiful girl, June. Do not tempt me."

I ran, stumbled, sort of lurched forward away from my car to get closer to him. "Don't leave without me, Nic. I know it's silly."

"What is silly are the people who never get to say these things. Or feel them."

Snowflakes drifted seamlessly down to the ground in a winter dance.

"I'm on my way to the airport, June."

"Then I'll drive you."

A smile formed on his face. He walked forward until he was standing right in front of me, so close his suit jacket brushed the backs of my hands. I looked up and his mouth was on mine. A perfect meeting of lips. The kind of kiss that makes you forget your name and slide into the hands pulling you tight. For months I'd dreamed of this moment. This right here. His fingers touched my shoulders, my neck, my chin... my god.

"June?" he said.

I looked up. He was still standing on the sidewalk, holding his cup of coffee, brow furrowed.

"Yes?"

"You have the most intense concentration. I always wonder what you must be thinking."

The wind blew across the open lot next door. My eyes traveled the distance, the flat stretches of brown grass and patches of dirt. All of that flatness suddenly bothered me. I wanted rolling hills and towering old apartment buildings. I shivered. I was standing outside in a Wisconsin winter with no coat.

"Why don't you get breakfast and come sit with me in the airport, June."

My eyelids fluttered and my stomach flipped. I was one step closer to my fine layer of dust.

sex. with kerouac.

long afternoons. in the room. next to the railroad tracks. jack pointed with a cigarette in his hand. he pointed at everything, like he was marking it for later. tall, broad, dark gypsy eyes. a real man's man but sugar coated inside. you know. the kind of man who asked for a drink of beer instead of just grabbing it and swallowing back the buzz meant for you. he talked endlessly about the differences between this coast and the east. his words like pages he'd ripped out of a book he wrote constantly in his mind. lovemaking was always in lowercase letters. not the kind of guy on a mission to please women. he had no idea what he was doing. what he knew was that he couldn't sit in his aunt's sunny kitchen one second longer. he had to get on the road. the east had tightened him into a small, indescribable box. scavenger angels howled inside his temple, slapping their bare breast, wild.

at night we'd lay on the mattress. on the floor. under the window. sharing bottles of beer that fizzed and popped in our silences. we talked about great new beginnings. of each person rising with a collective awe burned into their heart. we talked about liberty for all living things, not just the ones we assigned value to. all of our days were nights. his sheets smelled like old clothes with ink stains everywhere, a weird connect the dots that allowed him to master his universe. the constellation of jack. up there. glowing all night. obsessing over making it with girls who would never understand him. the floor was littered with ideas. discarded. he held on to the old ways even as he let go.

in these nights we abandoned who we were. stepped into the wide open space of that room. they don't serve redemption at the last supper anymore. i wanted to draw him. this way and that. lines reaching up to the cracked winter sky. high. we fled into brushstrokes of dew and sunrise. i needed those dark, brooding eyes watching my dreams. too much coffee, black. excitement hummed. light danced wildly in the afternoons. he was building an empire out of popsicle sticks and playing cards. decks stacked in our favor. odds, jack yelled from the other room. odds.

Tips

Tupelo Honey's real mom died when she was real small but she loved her. That's how she ended up out there in the sticks with Auntie Monster and her boyfriend, Thursgood. It was funny how someone named him Thursgood, like he worked in Washington or was a King, because mostly he was good for nothing. At home it was all crazy, all the time. Auntie Monster called herself a business owner but they weren't nothing but a bunch of hooch runners. They were hauling it or drinking it and whatever small amount of not crazy they had left in their brains was distilled a long time ago. But that place had a roof and walls. Or so they liked to remind her. Auntie and Thursgood had run off in the middle of the night in a frenzy of screaming and door slamming. The silence was nice but the shack was low on provisions.

Tupelo Honey put on her Sunday shirt and set off down the old, dirt path that led to the county line and that's how she found that dead man floating right side up, staring straight into the blazing gates of heaven. She'd never seen anything dead in all her life except maybe a bug or some furry thing squashed on the side of the road. The dead man's eyes bulged out like the nastiest sight you done laid eyes on. But here's the thing. He was so quiet out there, floating under a clear, blue Mississippi morning with all of those Jesus bugs racing past his head. There had probably never been a finer morning in Jackson County and he was too dead to see it and Tupelo Honey thought that was a real shame.

She stared at him, trying to figure out if she'd ever seen him before and got this terrible fear he might rise up out of the water and grab her arm. She was gonna run away from the floating dead man when her eyes, god help her, caught a glimpse of those shiny new Wing Tips on his feet and boy were they nice. All leather and polished and pointy toed, looking like they cost a pretty penny. So, her mind got to thinking about how if she could get those shoes she could take them and sell them for money. And that was a fine plan so she rolled up her good pants and stepped barefoot out into the water where mud squished up between her toes. She said a quick prayer in Jesus' name cause she was about to lift some shoes off a dead man and would need a nod from the Holy Ghost. She reached down sure as she pleased and tugged that wet shoelace. But the shoe was stiff and wet and she wrestled with it. The man kicked up a stink. She tugged hard. His body sloshed around in the water until the shoe came free and she tossed it onto the bank behind her. She leaned over again and tugged on the second one cause one shoe is useless unless it's a piece of art or something.

After she wrestled those shoes loose she took them over to the quiet, little boy in the house with the blue door off the boulevard. Then she walked right down to the Police station and asked the woman with big hair and pink fingernails if she could talk to Sheriff Dietrich. He saw her right off, but wasn't smiling, because policemen are trained not to smile.

"Sheriff, there's a problem," she said.

That didn't make him look any happier. "What's going on, Tupelo Honey?"

"See I was walking down that old path that cuts from our property down to the county line and there's a dead man floating out on that lake where the Canadian geese come to hang out in the Spring."

The Sheriff blinked. "What did you say?"

She sighed big and long and irritated and repeated what she'd just said.

"Are you saying you saw a dead body?"

"Yes, sir. Dead as you ever saw."

"Are you sure?" He knelt down and leaned in so close she could smell the bologna sandwich on his breath. "You're positive it wasn't just someone playing a prank?"

She thought about wrestling them shoes off of his big feet, knowing he was already up at the pearly gates with St. Peter trying to decide if he'd been naughty or nice and just kept that part to herself.

"He's floating out in the water, all bloated, staring straight up into the sun like it ain't burning holes through his eyeballs."

Sheriff put his hand on her shoulder and looked worried. "If you're telling the truth then I'll have to ride out with a deputy and if we get out there and there's nothing going on then you'll cost the taxpayers a lot of money."

"I would never steal from a taxpayer," she said real loud.

Sheriff stood up and said to the big woman, "Get Officer Harper in here. We're going to ride out and see what Tupelo Honey is talking about." He adjusted his gun belt and turned to her. "You can ride in my car."

She got to feeling all silly with excitement over riding in a real police car. The Sheriff let her ride in the middle and she pointed this way and that as Enoch Harper asked her questions and wrote the answers down in his little note pad. The Sheriff had no idea there was a bootlegger path back there and Tupelo Honey was kinda irked about having to reveal her secret path.

~

Aesop was a quiet boy. He liked flowers, gardenias and braiding his mother's hair. That was before the war, before his daddy went off that fine day in June and returned in a box. He remembered his mother out on the front porch; hand over her mouth, talking to those men who'd come to tell her the truth. The locusts buzzed in anticipation of evening and the cicadas chirped. The sight of his mother crying, which he'd never seen before made him want to mash up all of the bad things in the world until they were nothing but a fine dust that he'd blow away like he blew out the candles on his ninth birthday. Daddy never saw his tenth.

Aesop was a quiet boy. He liked candy wafers and the women on Sunday all dressed for church. It was early summer and the earth was moist with the yielding plenty that came after a wet spring. You couldn't sit on the ground on account of the fact that a dark stain would appear on your britches so he sat out in the patio chairs rocking, watching his mother inside. She didn't cry anymore but she stared out the kitchen window at the carriage house where Daddy's workshop was set up. Nothing had been moved. Not a wrench or pipe or Saturday Evening Post. That's just the way it was.

Until that day in July when bugs were singing and his mother was in the kitchen cleaning all of the pots and pans with bleach and the stinging in his nostrils was so awful that he walked out onto the front porch and watched the Robins all a flitter in the birdbath.

That odd little girl with the braids and buckteeth showed up, sneaking along the hedges. She asked him to keep an eye on a pair of shoes. Aesop was a quiet boy. The kind who could watch a pair of shoes and keep a secret for a long time. No one asked much of him. That crazy, little girl was like a crack of lightning in his life and made him smile. No one paid her any attention because her mama was dead and she lived out in the woods with a bunch of derelicts. He'd heard people around town talk about her when he was supposed to be buying flour for his mother.

"That poor little girl," they'd say. And he'd stop listening and imagine the rest. That was his favorite part. Filling in all of the blank spaces with more interesting things. Like that pair of shoes, damp and musty, that sat on the windowsill in his bedroom under the blazing sunlight. Little flecks of dust rose in streams of light like thousands of tiny angels hovering to get a better look. *Praise be to God*, his mother would say.

He imagined that maybe those shoes were his daddy's and the little bucktooth girl found them in what could only be explained as a divine act of mystery. He took them gently from the windowsill, setting them quietly on the hard wood floor. He slipped his foot inside where it was cold and made his sock wet. His mother had cleaned his room for the day, so she'd be downstairs polishing and scrubbing for a while and wouldn't bother him. He pulled off his wet sock, then the dry one and hid them both in the bottom of the clothes hamper, under the cloth used to wash behind his ears. Back at the windowsill he lifted the shoes again. The smell of lake soaked down into the soles, a smell so rich and black it spread out under everything, like the boogeyman, dark and unknowable.

Aesop was a quiet boy and lived up to this notion as he stepped barefoot into the shoes, first left, then right, riding back on his heels, just enough to lift the toes off of the floor. He imagined the sound of his daddy's footsteps on the stairs, calling out to his mother in a glorious roar, "I'm home, Sylvia. Where's my boy?" He imagined the very act of finding the shoes would draw his father back from the hereafter. It was then and there, Aesop knew he must hide them and never let them go.

~

Lara had known sorrow. It wasn't a bother to her. The world went on spinning. A big, dusty, round rock that hurled through outer space. It was something she thought about often. Outer space. Two of the most boring words in the entire human language spoke separately but once combined they became exotic, the stuff of mystery.

Outer space.

Most of the space in her present world was filled with the long dead furniture of Mr. Morris' deceased mother, god rest her soul. A wife was not in his destiny, he said, what with all of the work he did and getting up in the middle of the night and having to go out because the world had come undone. Mr. Morris said respectable women couldn't live under the same roof once they'd known what he'd seen. Lara hated the women who drowned their babies upside down in buckets of dirty water and the men who stabbed people until all of the blood ran out of their bodies and left them in the morgue. Mr. Morris had seen those things with his own eyes. That was why the Jim Beam bottle followed him from room to room. The bottle and Lara.

She reckoned she could wait a lifetime for a man like Mr. Morris to notice the pretty green flecks in her eyes and the way her white skin glowed all pretty in the late afternoon light. She wasn't an old maid yet. There was still time. So much of it. Time was another thing she considered on those mornings full of work. She imagined whole lives they'd never had together while she ironed his shirts, running her fingertips down the sleeves, lightly caressing the buttons, folding open the collars, unzipping the trousers. The bathroom smelled like shaving soap and Bay Rum. She inhaled deeply, polishing the faucets.

The places she wanted to visit cascaded through her mind. The seven wonders of the world. They could see them together, hand in hand.

Since her mama passed through the pearly gates no one waited on her to return home. They had been a small family. Then her mother fell down and Mr. Morris helped in every way, even carried her from the car into the house when she was discharged from the hospital.

The whole time Lara stared up into the night sky trying to remember names of the constellations. Then Mr. Morris called her name and the sound of his voice was like a beacon in the darkest night and she followed.

Now his birthday had come around. In the old days his mother fussed and fiddled, putting a small party together for her only son. She bought a nicely decorated triple layer chocolate cake from the Bakery and sent out invitations. It was nice. She was a good mother. But when she was gone, Lara realized that no one would be there to celebrate the day he was born. So, she made a secret trip downtown, wearing her navy coat and smart handbag. She wondered what in the world to buy until her eyes caught a glimpse of the perfect gift. A pair of Wing Tips sat on top of a display stand in the shoe department. A man needed a good pair of shoes. Sturdy, solid and attractive. A man needed a good pair of shoes to walk confidently into his future. She purchased the Tips on the spot and had the box wrapped in powder blue paper with a big silver bow.

On his way into work, Detective Morris drove past the house on the boulevard with the blue door but didn't stop. Some nights he parked his unmarked Ford ten blocks down behind Jackson Tire and from there walked the distance through shrubs and silence to Sylvia's back porch. She, too, waited in the shadows and when she saw him they slipped quietly into the carriage house out back. In the dim light of the hurricane lamp her skin glowed the color of warm cinnamon. Years passed in secret. Except before it was more complicated. Her husband had been alive, his mother, too. But the two obstacles to their future faded away and he snuck over often to see her. If anyone recognized him prowling around in the shadows, he said he was on official police business.

Even that would be different soon. They were going to move. All of them. Together. To the edge of Harlem where worlds converged and people didn't stare at the color of their skin and pinch the corners of their eyes up in disapproval. He had to think of the boy and his future. His boy. That strange, quiet boy who looked so much like him but with dark skin. He'd tried not to love her, for her sake and his mother's sake, but he'd been terrible at not loving Sylvia. Be careful who you love because you'll love them forever, his mother used to say. Truer words were never spoken. From the first time he'd seen Sylvia walking home from church when he was just seventeen, he'd loved her madly. Now she was a widow. And once you've married the wrong person and been set free you look upon the world with a bigger vision and a little hunger, which rumbled deep in his belly.

He looked down at the pot roast sandwich Lara packed in his lunch. The reports on his desk sat in a golden pool of lamplight. The station was quiet. At that hour most desks were empty. Lamps glowed on the desktops, making each one a private world, illuminated by a tiny star glowing in the dark of night. He shook his head, gave a little laugh, and thought that sounded like something Lara would say. His eyes drifted to the stack of reports. He'd spent all day running leads and come up with zero. The big black rotary phone on his desk rang. The metal spring on his chair groaned as he rolled forward to answer.

"Jackson County Sheriffs Department. Detective Morris speaking."

"What's buzzin, cuzzin?"

"Who is this?"

"Is this the heat?"

Detective Morris straightened in his seat. "Who is this?"

"Who I am doesn't matter jive daddy. Who I know is what makes a difference."

"Who do you know?"

"You know how you're always looking for those hooch runners filling up your county with Shine?"

"How do you know that?"

"Because I've seen you out there hoofing it in Nowheresville, man. Listen. You got something I want. I got something you want."

"What's that?"

"Tips."

"Tips?"

"Yeah, like where those hillbilly hooch runners are and how they're sneaking it down an old, dirt path straight to the county line. *Your* county line."

"How do you know?"

"Same way I know the sky is blue. I seen it."

Detective Morris shuffled papers around on his desk looking for something to write with. Finally, he flipped the top of his fountain pen off. "Give me directions. I'll drive over check it out."

The moon glowed high in the sky. Detective Morris pulled his unmarked Ford into a grove of trees, cut the engine and listened. Tree frogs and locusts hummed. Insects chirped skeet skeet skeet. The earth was soft. He looked down at his new Wing Tips. It was the first time he'd thought of anything other than busting up a Moon shine ring in the half an hour it took him to drive out to the woods, based on a tip from a slick mouth stranger trying to bust his cousin out of county jail.

Light from the dashboard reflected off his shiny Wing Tips. A more practical man would have the sense to keep a spare set of shoes in the trunk. Barefoot was not an option. Hell, if he ruined them, he'd drive down to the department store and buy a new pair, so as not to hurt Lara's feelings. His eyes adjusted to the dark silhouette of leaves under the light of a full moon. He closed the door to the Ford gently, certain he knew how to cut down the path by the lake without getting lost. The slick mouthed stranger delivered detailed instructions during the call. He was hot to get his cousin out. Morris was hot to bust up a Shine ring and get the letter of recommendation needed to transfer to a precinct in Harlem.

The woods darkened until he passed the lake with the tree frogs covering up the sound of his footsteps with their loud, ancient song. He was sure he'd walked more than a mile when a lamplight flickered in the distance. He slowed to a stop, his ears trying to discern each sound. Footsteps, bottles clanking, car doors opening and closing. He pressed forward, to the edge of the wood, where he saw plain as day, a lamp in the window of an old shack. He patted his hip several times before realizing in his haste he'd left his gun belt back at the station, hanging on his chair. He bent over to pull his backup .38 Special from a leg holster when he heard a single twig snap. Morris rose up fast, flashed his badge. The dark figure of a man watched.

The wind blew against Morris' ear, and a Whip-poor-will broke into its haunting song. Then the hard blow of a pipe wrecked his brain. He stumbled, turned, and was smacked again harder. His nose burned, blood filled his mouth. He allowed himself to fall to the ground and reached for his holster until he heard the crack of his own skull and felt the pain rush down his arm in a thunderous rage. By now he realized there was more than one dark figure. He tried to tell them he was on official police business, to put his hands in the air, but the words mixed with blood in his throat and gurgled, until he sputtered and closed his eyes. An image of Sylvia filled his mind. He could see her standing, bright and pretty in a white dress with tiny blue birds flying around the hem. The rich, brown of her skin glowed copper in the fading sunlight. She held out her hand to him as she called to their son. But he could not reach her and his eyes drifted to the lightning bugs, hovering and flickering above the lush mid-summer grass. He felt a dark stranger pull his gun from the holster, then drag him along the path. Rocks dug into his shoulder blades but he could not move. Some deep, hidden fear in him rose up. Off in the distance he heard the sound of a little girl singing and he begged with all his strength, please find my boy. Tell him I'm coming home.

Roommates

{the Shepherd}

The Clash plays full volume, every morning at 7AM. Rock the Casbah rocks the walls. In a former life his ancestors were shepherds and tended to flocks. In modern times he herds bad kids all night at the runaway shelter. His vocabulary is massive. He carries a baseball bat to work. His car is a motorcycle. He wants to be famous and giving credit where credit is due he does look like a young Peter Fonda.

Chicks dig him.

The last chick of the day is pregnant. The current chick is not. The roommates have been instructed to be quiet regarding this fact, feign ignorance, shrug, pretend to be deaf. Just whatever you do, don't talk to new girlfriend about old girlfriend. Seriously. The drama with the rest of the roommates is enough to deal with. The Shepherd has to get an operation. He is very vague with the details. Exceedingly vague. Post Op he sits with a bag of frozen peas on his crotch. Another roommate thinks it's a gonad problem. A rumor erupts. Gonad removal. We are sure.

The Shepherd eats my leftovers. When I confront him, empty paper carton in hand, he shrugs, tells me I eat at all of the good restaurants. Butt kisser. He tells me I'm not like the other roommates. He is trying to ingratiate, insinuate his way into my lo mein box.

I am not falling for this. Like I said, chicks dig him. There's a pregnant one downstairs to prove it. The shepherd does not clean the bathroom sink or vacuum but he does steal cigarettes if you leave your pack on the breakfast bar in Community Sector One. Community Sector One is a combo of the kitchen and dining area. Don't even think about leaving something in the living room. The coffee table is the Bermuda Triangle.

On weekends we go to really trendy bars, drink overpriced Irish whiskey and play fight club in the front yard until we are so bruised and stupid we can barely move. Our neighbor is the police department. Cops come and go, day and night, at the Police Resource Center. The Shepherd is not concerned. All of his drugs are prescribed by people who went to go to college and have initials after their names. The Shepherd's father paid a lot of money for him to study psychology so he could pretend to have a host of disorders and get drugs. Legal drugs. One night over a bottle of 18 year Scotch that cost as much as our rent, he takes the drugs because he's a shepherd without a flock. The alcohol picks at his brain. I can see it. Chicks are his flock as far as I can tell but they roam. That presents a problem.

The old girlfriend is in the Shepherds room waiting for her appointment to terminate her pregnancy. The other roommates are annoyed by her presence. Her predicament proves life is messy. We all agree they must have been doing it to the Clash. *Rock the Casbah.* He tells us in a hushed whisper the old girlfriend still loves him.

I say, "If she loved you then she'd have your baby. You're delusional."

He buys her Chinese food after the termination. He says it's the least he can do. Collectively we stand in Community Sector One and roll our eyes. The roommates believe he only has one gonad left, thus diminishing future procreation abilities. Get it while you can. That's the prevailing sentiment. The old girlfriend goes back to the place where old girlfriends go.

The new one arrives. We like her. She is sweet and demure and educated in Europe. We stand in Community Sector One with her and drink coffee until she asks us what we've been doing. A tension seizes the group. Um, uh umm uh, we say intelligently. The Shepherd herds her off to drink overpriced Irish Whiskey and not mention the baby that he didn't have. A few nights later he calls at 1 AM. He says he doesn't feel so good. His arm hurts, he's sweating, can't catch his breath.

Heart attack, I say.

No, he says. No way, he repeats. "I'm only twenty-six."

Heart attack, I say.

He does not believe me. Finally, he agrees to let me take him to the emergency room which is horrifically ugly and bright. The most awful doctor in the world interrogates him.

Then the doctor starts in on me. Can I talk to you, he asks.

Sure, I say, to this totally clueless prick.

How much cocaine has your friend had, he asks.

What?

How much cocaine?

None.

I can't help your friend if you're not truthful with me. How much cocaine?

Fuck you, I say. He was at work.

The conversation is over. The power tripping MD storms off.

An hour later the Shepherd has another heart attack at the hospital and now they believe him. He stays for days. I sit next to his bed reading passages from As I Lay Dying, at his request. Finally a different doctor comes in and tells him the infection he had in his upper respiratory system moved to his heart.

Creepy.

He is discharged and made to swear on a stack of bibles that he'll leave red meat and cigarettes alone. Forever. After three days he is such an asshole that I threaten to perform CPR with lungs full of cigarette smoke if he doesn't get a patch. He buys a pack of Camels instead.

When we get home the Crazy Girl is crying, screaming, being a drama queen.

"What the fuck is wrong with her?" the Shepherd yells.

"She's crazy," I say.

None of us know what's wrong with her. A week later she tries to commit suicide. Her sister comes to pick up all of her stuff. She tells us the crazy girl is in an institution.

"Didn't see that one coming." The Shepherd rolls his eyes.

Now we have the entire downstairs to ourselves until my brother dumps his girlfriend.

The Shepherd and I go out for dirty, wet martinis.

"Have you ever been in love?" I ask.

"Why? Are you going to drink too much and tell me you love me?"

"No. I was wondering if you love someone."

He eats honey and bread. "Maybe."

"Maybe has nothing to do with love."

"How do you know?" he asks, flagging down a server.

I order a double whiskey on ice. Conversations about love are always on the rocks.

He leans in, confessing, "I have something to tell you."

"Are you going to drink too much and tell me you love me?"

"I took the job in Japan."

"Deserter. I can't believe you're leaving me alone with those lunatics."

"I knew you'd bring that up."

"So, what's your girlfriend going to do?"

"She says she'll wait but really she'll find a new boyfriend."

"And you?"

"I look forward to the madness of Tokyo."

"The Japanese are going to be terrified of you."
"All the more reason to go."

{the Chef}

On his day off Hank Williams Sr. blares from his crappy, plastic stereo balanced on a stack of unpacked boxes. His room is directly above The Shepherds. Hey good looking does not Rock the Casbah. The Chef is a shiny, dark Italian with gypsy eyes. He cooks Tortelloni a la zucca and Ragu a la bolognese at Del Cambio Ristorante. The first night I meet him he tells me he lived in a homeless shelter with his dad who'd had an aneurysm. A year later his dad was well enough to get a job. They got a trailer. The Chef got a girlfriend. Then the girlfriend got a girlfriend. So the Chef did the same. When she found out he'd screwed someone else the first girlfriend smashed his guitar. He took it like a man. He threw her clothes out the front door of the trailer. Eight months later he had a son. Then he met a nice hippie girl named Rose who dished out a sexually transmitted disease. Not the keep your dick in your pants a few weeks kind. The kind that never goes away. In exchange for free rent Rose left the Chef with festering blisters on his manhood. Then she blew out of town with no forwarding address. It's funny what people will tell you. The crazy girl has a crush on the Chef. We all know it. She walks around, saying, "We're not going to have any secrets in this house."

The Shepherd tells her to shut up. The Chef has stopped smoking dope and started reading. His inquisitive nature is unmasked. He wants to know everything about me. He walks from the shower to his bedroom naked. I'm pretty sure it's an invitation to stare. He shows me photos of his son. I have never considered having children. It is all so weird to me.

"You're not even old enough to buy beer," I say. Suddenly, beer is such a qualifier. No beer. No kids. *How can someone who isn't old enough to buy beer have such grown up problems?*

"I'm old enough to buy cigarettes," he says.

"That's reassuring."

"They'll be no secrets in this house," the crazy girl says.

The Chef cooks me dinner. Greens wilted in vodka, roasted Portobello mushrooms. The house is empty. It's weird. I drink my wine, twirling my glass between my fingers. I am thinking that people who are not old enough to buy beer should not be old enough to have kids.

"So what are we doing here?" I ask to change the subject in my mind.

"You make me feel so stupid," he says.

"You cooked me dinner because I make you feel stupid?"

"No, not that," he says, cryptically.

"Let's talk about something else." He tells me his ex-girlfriend is trying to take his son away. Because I've had two glasses of wine, I am sure she cannot do this. I am sure he must not let her remove his name from his son's life. I look at him in the candlelight of Community Sector One and wonder why he isn't hiking across a campus on his way to American Lit or eating a bowl of ice cream. Why does he have such grown up problems? How did someone not old enough to buy beer end up with such massive, life changing decisions.

After an uncomfortable pause, I ask, "What do you know about the guy in the Basement?"

He thinks a minute. "Nothing really."

"How is it you can live in a house and not know anything about someone?"

"Because all I want to know about him is that he pays rent, on time, every month."

"How did you find him?"

"He answered the ad for a roommate."

"And that's it?"

"Pretty much."

"What if he's down there hiding body parts?"

"Makes no difference to me. Rent money," he adds, winking.

Eventually my two and a half glasses of wine go to my head. "I have to go to my room," I say.

"Okay," he says.

And that is that. I am sure I missed something. Maybe not. I am sure that was a date but don't want to be too assuming. I go to see a psychic. The psychic describes the Chef, says he lives upstairs from me and that I will hurt him. He says it's Karmic, that we have known each other in past lives and that we will not fix our problems with each other in this life.

"That's cheerful," I say.

Then the psychic tells me not to move to Texas.

Okay.

"Do not move to Texas," he repeats.

The Chef has no matching furniture, no matching sheets or clothes. Everything he owns looks like it was a hand me down. His room is messy, covered in cat fur. He keeps marijuana hidden in a drawer in his closet. Sometimes when he's at work I sneak into his room and sit on his bed. This spawns rumors in the house but I don't care. It's not what they think.

The Chef has the best view in the house. When you sit in the middle of his bed you can see the mountains perfectly through the windows that line an entire wall. Those crazy mountains. Weirdest thing to see. I grew up in Mississippi next to a wide crack in the earth filled with water.

I don't even know where I am when I look through these windows.

One day, I fall asleep. A simple, I'll just close my eyes for a minute, nap. Six hours later it is dark in the room. The Chef is sitting on the bed. Into the dark night, he says, "Are you okay?"

I nod, but it's not very convincing.

He turns to look at me, his dark gypsy eyes wet with tears. His soul is windswept.

The next day his son comes to visit. He is a dark haired replica of the Chef but smaller. He screams and screams, red faced, tiny fists clenched. The Shepherd begs me to go with him to the New French Bar and drink whiskey. "I can't stand to hear babies cry," he says.

I roll my eyes, thinking of the last girlfriend. "I know," I say.

My brother breaks up with his girlfriend and she starts hanging out at my house. One night I come home and the house is quiet. No one appears to be home. While I'm downstairs I hear footsteps upstairs. Twenty-minutes later my brother's ex comes downstairs.

"Where have you been," I ask?

"Out," she says.

"Liar," I say.

Three days later she is really sick. The Chef is strangely absent. I drive her to the health department. Five hours later I pick her up. She is crying. It seems the STD gift has been given again. Her fever is 103 and she is sweating profusely, feverish, delirious. The Shepherd takes care of her while I drive to Del Cambio Ristorante. I ask someone carrying crates of vegetables to go in and find him. If I go inside I'll make a scene. He comes out and gets into my car. We sit in silence under the streetlamps. I can hear him breathing. I am so mad I think that if I say one word I am going to explode, so I say nothing. Minutes pass on the digital clock on my dashboard. Each number replaced by a new one, a different one and you can't get the old number back.

Abruptly, I say, "Do you know why I'm here?"

I watch him, mentally daring him to do anything that will justify me slapping his face. His lips tighten.

After a few seconds, he says, "Just because I like you doesn't mean...I mean, we're not dating. I can sleep with other people. If you're not going to date me then you can't be jealous."

I look at him and say, "If you'd really been sleeping then I wouldn't have had to pick her up from the health department today."

The color drains from his face. Again, silence.

"It was so fast though," he says.

"It usually is. How many times?"

"Twice."

Now he looks at me. I see him in the moonlight, this person who has stood by everything I've done since meeting him and my heart softens a bit even though I try to resist.

"Does she know about me?" he asks.

"No. But I do," I say. "No one knows I'm here. I'm going to leave the rest up to you. You're going to have to work this out. You're going to have to do the right thing."

He looks at the ceiling of my car, reaching for the door handle. "I have dinner orders piling up inside."

I watch him walk underneath the warm buttery glow of the streetlamps and my heart breaks in a way I can't ignore.

Three days pass. I check his room. I call his work.

Sick, they say.

Yeah, right, I say.

On the fourth day the Chef appears and makes dinner for everyone.

"What are you doing?" I demand.

"The only thing I know how to do," he says.

"You don't seriously think preparing food is going to fix everything, *do you*?"

He stares at me. Finally, he says, "I didn't know I was going to meet you. I didn't know I was going to love you." His eyes brim with tears. "This just wasn't what I planned."

I am so mad. I hold my breath, grind my teeth. Just to get some air, I say, "This is so unacceptable."

He follows me into Community Sector One and lays his hand on my shoulder.

"Stop," I say.

"Mistakes. That's all I seem to make," he says.

"Have you lost your mind?"

He shakes his head.

"What are you going to do?"

"What can I do?" He shrugs.

"I don't know. *Fix this*."

Neither of us says anything. We just stand there listening to the guy from the basement and the shepherd playing fight club outside.

Finally, he says, "What can I do." A resignation. Not a question. "I can't undo this," he says, matter-of-factly.

"Then what? This is just another imperfect day in paradise?"

"You're acting like someone has done something to you."

Anger flushes into my cheeks. "No. I'm just asking why."

"Why?" he repeats, raising his eyebrows. "The why is easy. Lonely people do dumb things."

"So, lonely people commit random acts of stupidity. That's how this happened?"

"I begged her to let me wear a condom—"

"You're not even old enough to buy beer," I scream.

The front door swings open, banging against the wall. I turn.

The guy from the basement jerks his thumb toward the driveway. "The crazy girl took a bunch of pills and washed it down with a bottle of tequila."

The chef and I run outside. A siren wails in the distance. The crazy girl stumbles around, incoherently in the front yard. Her shirt is down around her waist, exposing her breasts. The guy from the basement runs over to her, then grabs his nose, backing away.

"What?" I yell.

The crazy girl reaches for him.

Basement stumbles backyards. "She rolled in dog shit."

She turns around, like a dog chasing its tail, to look. Her back is smeared with a dark brown goo.

The ambulance turns into the driveway, screeching to a halt. A Medic jumps out. The crazy girl spins again, but this time she goes down for the count. The lights from the ambulance flash over her breasts, bulbous and strange, surrounded by grass, as she lays on her back, staring blankly at the stars.

{the guy in the basement}

No one knew anything about the guy in the basement. Including me. All I knew was that every morning there was some guy in the kitchen making a pot of green tea and oatmeal. He'd smile and say, "Good morning."

"We have a basement?" I ask.

"Yeah, it's under the house," the crazy girl says.

The Shepherd has the most information on the guy in the basement because the door to the hall that leads to the stairs that lead to the basement connects through the Shepherd's room.

"What's he doing down there?" I ask.

"He makes Zen pillows and goes around to all of the dumpsters at night to get food the stores throw out."

"There's a guy stuffing Zen pillows in the basement?"

"As far as I know."

I turn into Sherlock Holmes. I ask all of the roommates about the guy in the basement. No one knows. I sneak down to the back of the house. I am sure it is a grim, dark place full of dragons. No such luck. In fact it's not even a real basement with dark, dank corners. It is actually the first floor of the house. It is ground level with windows on two sides. I peer through the windows like a peeping Tom. It's actually kind of cheerful.

I walk back inside and knock on the Shepherds door. "I want to see the basement."

"Sure." He points his baseball bat at a door across the room. I open the door and descend into the basement. From where I am standing on the staircase I can see a neat little palette of blankets on the floor with a heater next to it, stacks of zen pillows in various stages of creation and an extremely bright, tidy dungeon.

Basement walks around the corner and looks up at me. My cheeks flush hot.

"Hey," I say.

He smiles. "Hey."

"Do you live in the basement?"

"Yeah."

"What do you do down here?"

"Think. Stuff pillows. Write down ideas. I've been making some really cool sculptures."

"Really? Can I see them?"

"I took them downtown to have them fired but I'll get them back in a few days."

"Where are you from?"

"San Francisco."

"You're from California?"

"Yeah. Where are you from?"

"I guess I'm from a lot of places but I moved here from Wisconsin. How did you end up here?"

"I went to the airport and bought a ticket for the next flight leaving. The ticket agent said Altamont, NC. So I bought a ticket, went home, packed up my stuff and came here. What are you doing here?"

I shrugged. "I was having an affair."

"Are you still having an affair?"

I shake my head.

"Why not?"

"Because it was so convoluted. Married guys can never get their act together."

Basement laughs. "Are you telling the truth?"

"Of course I am. It's too stupid to make up."

"Why do you think people cheat?"

"Because they're afraid to be alone so they hold on with one hand and reach out with the other. What about you? What are you getting away from?"

I expect him to hesitate, stutter, lie.

Not basement. He looks me directly in the eye and says, "My dad's a total mental case."

"Like annoying nut job or certifiably crazy?"

"More certifiable. He thinks people are watching him."

"They are."

Basement laughs. "I don't know. Maybe."

I sit down on the stairs and we talk for hours. I learn loads of information. I learn his favorite childhood toy. Fischer Price record player. Favorite color. Dark purple. Favorite food. Caramel apples. Anyone who eats caramel apples can't be that bad.

Two days later the Crazy Girl starts screaming and wailing.

"Tell that bitch to shut up," the Shepherd yells, pointing his baseball bat at her.

Because I can't take the madness I ask her what's wrong. She hugs herself tightly and tells me that boys don't like fat girls.

I go to a Sufi dream workshop. Basement comes with me. The workshop is on the top floor of a brightly lit yoga studio. In a room full of strangers we reveal our dreams, the hidden symbols locked deep in our psyche. We meditate, breathe, descend, explore, examine, rise. I look around the room. The winter afternoon drifts. It is serene, quiet, dreamy, so cold outside that I want to fall asleep. Day turns to night and we leave. Beauty exists. I am sure of it. The world is so quiet, the streets so vacant, like the city has been abandoned. We drive back to the house unwilling to undo the silence we've built. Stars shine in a cold night.

"Thanks," Basement says before he descends the stairs. 'I would have never known about that without you."

Immediately I recall a passage from Rumi. "My soul is from elsewhere, I'm sure of that, and I intend to end up there."

A few days later Basement is making green tea in his glass pot. I stagger sleepily up the stairs and around the corner to find him there. He is so cheerful in the mornings. I am moving in a thick, dim haze trying to make coffee. I was out late rocking the casbah.

"How did you sleep?"

I look over. "Okay. It's so damp here."

"San Francisco is wet and cold. It's not too different."

I grunt in agreement.

"The Chef likes you," he says, grinning like a goofy lunatic.

The mention of something so silly wakes me up a little.

"The Chef has a pile of personal problems," I say, willing my coffee to brew faster. "I don't think he'll be adding me to that pile anytime soon."

"I see the way he looks at you. It's quite impressive."

"Impressive how?"

"Because I'd like for someone to look at me the way he looks at you."

"Like what?" I press.

"Like he loves you and he is afraid to say it."

"So you want someone to love you and be afraid to say it?"

He laughs, then points out the obvious. "Your coffee is ready."

After tea and coffee are poured and sipped he says, "My statues are ready. Do you want to go with me to pick them up?"

I nod.

Basement stacks boxes of seated Buddhas into the back of his truck with the rebel flag painted across the tailgate. I wait in the front seat, thinking about how I arrived here in the first place.

{the narrator}

The big question is: what am I doing in this house full of roommates? Everyone wants to know how I ended up here? I met the Crazy Girl at a party. That's how. My lease was up on my apartment and I was wandering...

But wait. Back up. There's this really important thing that happened before. Dr. Murphy made me take a test. It was the only test I'd failed in my life. It flat out scared the crap out of me. I was sent to the Health Department because I failed a tuberculosis test. Long, putrid green corridors led me to an elevator that descended into the bowels of the establishment. I failed three tests. I was sent for X-rays. A mean spirited nurse informed me that if any spots showed up on my lungs I'd be quarantined and forbidden to leave.

"We'll call whoever you want to pick up your car," she said, sucking down the last of her diet Coke.

There were no spots on my lungs and I was allowed to leave.

The next day I went to the movies to see Moulin Rouge. I was Satine. At the end of the movie she dies of tuberculosis. I felt cast adrift from what I'd known before. Now I was in this weird little Southern town acting out parts of movies.

So I meet the Crazy Girl at a party and when I need a place to live the Crazy Girl says I can come stay at her house. She has a huge room that we section off and share. Under normal circumstances I wouldn't agree but since I have TB it doesn't matter anymore. The Chef moves all of my furniture. My rent is officially eighty dollars a month. I am cold all of the time. The cold in this place is never ending. The Crazy Girl begins to cry because the Chef is ignoring her. One night The Chef puts his arms around me in Community Sector One and she sees us. She slams the front door on the way out.

This makes me mad and I follow her out, yelling across the front yard, "What's wrong with you?"

She stops at her Volkswagen convertible. It is so dented you can't imagine how it was ever whole. She watches me a minute. Her dark hair shines in the moonlight. Her ass is so big it covers the shadows.

Finally, she opens her car door and yells, "We were going out before you came along."

"Who?"

She points at the living room window. I turn and see the dark silhouette of the Chef watching us.

"Oh, Christ," I say, walking back inside. "This isn't junior high."

I slam the door. The Chef is ten feet away. "Are you going out with her?"

"It was only sex. Before my problem."

"You had sex with her?"

He regards me seriously a moment. "Are you going to hit me?"

"Why?"

"Jealousy?"

"What would I have to be jealous about? She's crazy."

"Come here," he says.

I walk into his arms.

"Come watch the moon rise over the mountains with me," he says.

We walk to his room carrying a bag of blueberry muffins and a bottle of wine. At first he plays love ballads on his guitar that make me smile. I lay in his lap and the warmth of his chest so broad and strong and the glaze of the wine makes me tell him my secret.

"You're dying," he whispers, leaning forward to see my face.

"Maybe," I say.

"How do you stop it?"

"I don't. I can't take the drugs."

It is so quiet. The room is awash with blue light from the moon.

That night a fine white powder drifts down from the sky. I wake, still in my clothes, next to the Chef. Outside it is a winter wonderland. We drink bottles of Pinot Noir and read Rumi's poems in the moonlight.

"You should stop smoking," he says.

I raise my eyebrows. "Really? What's the point now?"

He shrugs.

I begin driving to the top of a mountain every night after midnight to listen to the BBC. If I'm going to die then I want to get pissed off at all of the political bullshit I tried to accept before. I want to stand up on top of a mountain and get mad. First the first time in my life I wonder what it would be like to be in love. Really in love. Under a cascading spray of moonlight, I think about true love. Wonder and awe descends upon me. I listen to the sound of the rain, to my heartbeat, to the sounds of crows calling from tree to tree. I am crushed beneath the sorrow of leaving this magnificently sparkling, bent, beautiful, honeysuckle filled world behind.

{epilogue}

The night before Basement goes back to San Francisco him and the Chef and I take acid. A cold February night darkens the edges around us. Together we place squares of acid on each other's tongues like members of a secret club. We hang around the house until the walls begin shrinking. Basement is terrified he'll go insane, that he dive over the edge and forget how to get back. I tell him that he'll be okay. He asks me to hold his hand. I do. We are watching The Matrix in the basement when the ceiling begins breathing and Neo steps out of the television. I am distracted by a toilet in the back corner of the basement. No partition. No curtain. Just a toilet.

I ask Basement if he ever uses it and he says, "Sure. All of the time." I'm certain that to use a toilet you must also close a door. "Not so," he says, "young grasshopper. I am proof." We discuss the toilet until the Chef comes looking for us.

The night is so dark. I have a copy of 1984. I read passages aloud until we are sure the end of privacy is near. We drive high into the mountains to escape the think police in my shiny new, red car that I will bequeath to my brother when I am dead. Our altitude is determined solely by how far I can drive. My headlights bounce across the road like a disco. I pull off of the road on a grassy shoulder.

We're a team the Chef says.

Okay, we're a team.

We stay together, he says.

We get out and find a path that runs along the steep face of the mountain. With only moonlight to light our way we set off into the wilderness. The path is narrow. I stop and sit on the ground. I don't notice that it's cold. I don't notice that I'm not wearing a coat. I only notice the face of the night I am staring into. I look back toward my car and that's when I see it. A man crouched down in between me and my car smoking a cigarette. His profile glows in the moonlight, ominously. The profile of a man. He turns, looks at me, his eyes narrow. I know I will have to pass him on the path in order to get back to my car. I have forgotten about the others. I listen for the golden embers burning on the end of his cigarette. I listen for the sizzle. A cold dead silence fills the air. I need to get back to my car. He is blocking my way, waiting like a big cat waits. I can't remember how long I've been here. It feels like minutes but could be hours. I have to get back to my car. I have to get out of this place. I can fight him if I have to. He is not real. I can get past him. He begins to fade. *He is not real.* The burning ember of his cigarette becomes a house light far in the distance. I turn back to the mountain that drops down to the bottom of the earth. Indians rise up in the mist, bare chested, with war paint, and feathered headdresses. They rise. They are ethereal, light, released from the soil. Each one rises, lingers in the cold air, like an army of my ancestors. I stand up on the trail. The Indians watch me. I look back to my car. The man has completely disappeared. The Indians break up like smoke, their images pulled apart, disappearing. I look around, listening.

When I hear nothing I call out, "Where are you?"

I hear a giggle. The Chef says, "Over here."

"Over where?"

"Up the trail. Beyond the rise."

Our voices echo in the odd still air.

"What are you doing?"

"Building a fort," Basement says.

"I think we should all be together," I say.

I hear footsteps on the path, then they crest the top, moonlight shining down on their faces. I look back and see that the Indians and the man are gone. The psychedelics are leaving my bloodstream. The three of us sit on the path and talk about the lies the media pushes. Now that I can drive we get in the car and drive all of the way to the top of the mountain.

A sapphire, blue light glows in the east. A dark valley, sprinkled with lights, spreads out beneath us. We have been listening to Kid Rock all night. A song plays on the car stereo. The doors are open. Kid Rock is taking us to the river. The Chef thinks it's the best song he's ever heard. His face is practically glued to the speakers.

Finally Basement says, "Let's make a pact to take over the world. The three of us."

I let out a loud southern girl whoop and say, "Let's do it."

The Chef joins in.

Basement's eyes flicker in the naked dawn.

After our pact we get back in the car and drive back into the valley. Basement picks up his suitcases. He's leaving. Going back to San Francisco. Back to where he came from. He's done with the mountains, the basement, the Zen pillows, the Buddhas and the rebel flag.

We pile into the car. Team Psychedelic. I miss the exit for the airport and drive 125 miles per hour down the highway trying to get him there before his plane takes off. Even 125 MPH can't make up for the time lost. His plane leaves without him. We are outlaws. Real Outlaws. The kind that ride into sunrises.

The airline puts him on the next flight out. He hugs me, tells me how much I rock out loud. He is going home. This place is not home for any of us. I get in my car and pull away from the curb. Basement walks up to the sliding doors and disappears. I know I'll never see him again.

It is 7:54 AM. A cool, blue light shines from the East. I look out at this magnificent world. I imagine that we are the only ones that exist, that we have come to this planet at this very moment when the sun is rising. We are here digging deep down into our souls while colors assemble around us. We have been on a journey all night. There is so much in this moment. I am not the only one who feels it. The silence of the cold, still, winter dawn is stunning.

The house is empty when I arrive. A letter with a Japanese postmark is on the breakfast bar. I open it, make coffee, read. The entire note is written in Japanese. The only English is the closing, which reads: Live long and prosper, the Shepherd. Prosper, yes. Live long, maybe not. I never told him my secret. I lean back in my chair and think about skipping town. I imagine the stories people will tell. They will make up details. They will romanticize these days and nights. They will tell their friends that one day I just disappeared. It will be the truth.

Summer of Absalom

Sun melted in surrender around the warm glow of our bodies that first summer we spent together. In a small town in Mississippi we fell into each other's arms.

The sound of my aunt Louisa reading Faulkner aloud under the pale light in August drove him wild, the past echoing in her gently, lilting voice. A crack in the earth filled with water swooped off beyond the bluff into sunset. Hot, wild fragrant nights were book ended by dust floating down to tabletops. He strummed his six string and made my thighs long to be plucked, long to lay in his lap turning harmonic pages into song. Everything in my aunt's house was old, with a crank. No wireless, no hi-tech. A lonesome world, recreated every afternoon. No shiny distractions to tear me away from his smile.

Everything turned off at night, except us. I liked the way he called me baby even though the windows of his soul were dirty, streaked with the fingerprints of flawed gods, whiskey rhyming men full of swagger. Under the glow of a hurricane lamp our magnetic attraction for one another crackled like lightning out on the wide open plains.

Auntie read Faulkner while we snuck around all night falling in love with each other, breathing the still, balmy air. I whispered to him, laying next to me in bed and he smiled, laughed, kissed me. His kisses were like a good bottle of scotch. I never got enough of them. Never loved kissing anyone but him, not in my whole life. No one owned him, he'd never been a walking shadow. A bit of madness, trueness in his voice lured me in. Lonely, consumed out under the bright, blue sky a fierceness in his eyes swept me across the landscape. In the last fading rays of twilight we disappeared into the shadows of the parlor, far from my napping aunt.

A naked searching for feelings just below our skin exposed our layers to the world. Our hands were a wild catalog of exploration. If we slipped deep enough then quiet moans erupted and his fingers pressed against my lips. We retreated down to the boathouse in the hot, tomblike air breathing in the scent of jasmine blooming beneath the window.

The scent of me blooming in his hands.

On Wednesdays he went to see his uncle Ringo as he lay dying in the old folks' home. Afterwards we'd light stars with our fingertips, call sunsets into being. Storms rolled across the dusty plains. We fled into our warm bodies and listened. The sound of his footsteps on the hard, wooden planks of the front porch was divine music to me, divine in the way that bodies never leave love behind but yearn for it, are driven to find it hiding in the eaves.

We found an old treasure map when we stowed away in a closet. We stole shovels from the boathouse and endeavored to find treasure.

Into the dusty back roads went until we rounded a bend, on that dusty back road, and saw a man hanging from a tree. Flies flew in and out of his open mouth. White lips, eyes bulging. He looked over our heads in the direction of his murderer, an image burned onto his mind's eye but he could not curl his tongue around a name, could not climb down from the hereafter. The stink of the man kicked up in the breeze mingling with gardenia.

We vanished into the trees. Into the half light of August we went, unaided, alone. The sheriff came. They rode out on horses because the path was too narrow for cars, too far from the road. Thick, warm air clung to our arms. A deputy cut the man down but the rope still hung, ends frayed. We stared at those frayed ends, streams of sunlight rippling through the branches.

Uncle Ringo threw a vase of roses against the wall. I shook my head. Yankees won't go calmly to take the hand of God. Won't follow the devil straight to hell like everyone else.

When the last fallen rays of summer departed we slowed down into dreams of humble means, patched together with seams that connected intricate lives. The heat inside me was enough to light up the atmosphere. We tried so hard by not trying at all. It didn't have to make sense anymore. We went back to the place we'd come from because we'd never been there before. I drank too much Cabernet and tears rushed onto the kitchen tile as I railed against the end of summer, the frayed end of the man in the tree.

I went down to old man Zephron's cabin and he gave me a powder to drink under a full moon. When we kissed a vision would come, streaked with the fingerprints of flawed gods, whiskey rhyming men full of swagger. And with this we went unaided, alone, into the last days of summer crying *Absalom, Absalom.*

Figs

"Cotton," my grandmother yelled from the back porch. "Where are you, child?"

The back steps were rotting so she wouldn't dare come looking for me. For a while I'd pretend not to hear, but eventually I'd be forced to cross that great expanse of backyard from past to present. The family dog, Oswald, named after Lee Harvey, was always waiting on me. A neighborhood cat had kittens in the old washing machine in the basement. Now she'd moved them under the porch. They were feral. "Just like you," my Grandmother said.

She'd just bought a glass table that had fallen off the back of a truck. Everything in the house was stolen, including the medication. Uncle Stan was at the table eating Thorazine, green beans and fried chicken. I looked down at the drummie on my plate.

"What's wrong?" Granny asked, mashing potatoes.

"Nothing."

"She's been back there eatin' them figs all day, Mother." Stan said, smothering everything on his plate in a warm gravy.

"Have not."

"Have to. I seen you."

"Well, that's okay," Granny said. "Adam and Eve ate figs."

"Shoulda eaten snake," Stan said, pleased with himself.

That evening I climbed up on the old porcelain sink in the bathroom and stared down at the tree. It was as old as the Bible. It grew in faraway lands. Somehow it had made its way across a vast sea to our backyard.

"Cotton, how many times have I told you not to climb up on that sink? It's going to come loose from the wall."

I shimmied down the porcelain with a frown.

"What is it with you and that tree?"

"Where did it come from?"

"It was here when we moved in. A long time before you were born."

I was sure the tree had been taken from the Garden of Eden by a traveling salesman who rode on a magic carpet.

I stole the key to the old carriage house to look for clues. There was nothing out there except for dust, nails and a musty smell. I locked the padlock, put the key in my pocket and climbed the tree.

A bright blue calm day in the Empire. I picked honeysuckle flowers just to taste one drop of sweetness on my tongue. Then I ate a fig, sweet, tasty with its deep brownish, purple flesh and seeds. Twilight was upon me. The locusts began to sing a rhythmic song and the crickets chirped. I felt so high in the air, lingering next to the clouds.

Tomorrow it would rain and the ditch would swell like the Nile. I knew. I'd seen it before.

A Feeling

(in five acts)

i.

"It's a feeling," Eloise said.

"A what?"

"A feeling."

She didn't have time to finish the explanation because a small, robust woman piled items for purchase on the card table. I stared deep and hard at the feeling, taking in the details.

Eloise turned awkwardly in her fold out chair and rolled her eyes in a way that whispered *Philistine*, soft, yet final. "It's high art," she pressed.

And we left it at that.

Until the sale wound down. Stragglers came and went. Cars slowed but didn't stop. The feeling sat alone on an end table next to a set of golf clubs, lonely and out of place like a third grader trying to crash senior prom. The sky was overcast. Saturday. Occasionally a deal seeker actually stopped at the curb and jumped out of their car. It stunned me how ready people were to dig through the contents of someone else's life.

I contemplated the side bar and club chairs but mostly I stalked the feeling. Its slopes and tubes and the great open space in the middle. My peripheral vision remained keen and alert. If a yard saler came anywhere close I was ready to snatch it up and run to the card table. Until then, I was on the fence. I didn't exactly need a feeling, nor did I have any idea where I'd put one.

A red headed woman in a purple shawl and necklace big enough to sink the Titanic bought the Club Chairs out from under me. Which she paid too much for because she could have bought them online for half the price. That would have required her to use a computer which she admitted to Eloise was her least favorite way to shop.

"I like to touch things," she cooed in that way all computer illiterates do as she peeled off five and ten dollar bills.

I reached out while no one was looking and touched the feeling.

My fingers surfed the waves of its ripples and bumps, glazed ceramic cool to the touch.

Next went the golf clubs.

Divorce is messy.

The guy who bought the clubs got a chubby from his incredible find. "This totally makes up for the last fifteen yard sales I stopped at and didn't find a single thing," he beamed.

Swear to god.

Dream on, buddy.

The end does not justify the means.

Speaking of end, the end tables were still on the grass. Afternoon light slanted down, flirting with treetops. It was a perfect day to drag the contents of your broken home out onto the lawn and unload it on strangers.

People drove by but no longer stopped. Pickings were slim. A measly array of items lay strewn across the grass. Crank hand mixer, throw pillows, floor lamp.

Determined dark circles formed under Eloise's eyes. She closed the cash box and lifted the handle. "See anything you like? The friendship discount will be applied."

I pointed at the feeling.

Eloise thrust her hand out, palm up, "Pony up some cash."

I glanced at the price sticker. A blue dot with $120.25 was scribbled in the center.

"A hundred and twenty bucks is kinda pricey doncha think?"

She rolled her eyes. *Philistine.* "I made that with my bare hands."

The same ones wanting to be filled with cash.

"I'm on a budget."

"You're always on a budget."

"I'm smart. I have priorities."

"Your only priority is to swindle me out of my feeling at cutthroat prices."

It was true.

"How much money do you have?"

"Thirty-two dollars. But the thing is that I love these end tables and can put them to very practical use."

My boyfriend in college took my panties off during a riveting game of truth or dare. It wasn't like I was a virgin. I'd had sex before. Nothing weird. Standard fare. I'll show you mine if you show me yours. Watching him slide my panties down my thighs was admittedly kind of hot.

Then he put them in my mouth.

There are moments like this in life.

The ones where you can spit your panties out.

Or.

The *or* is too dirty to contemplate.

Fascinating opportunities to explore strangely erotic sides of your personality you never knew existed.

Because part of me liked it.

The other part knew I was never supposed to like anything that dirty.

It's like that with everything though.

The chocolate cream doughnut you're not supposed to eat. The hot guy you're not supposed to want. We are constantly at a crossroads of unexplained desires and irrational urges. Feelings that don't define who we are but instead kick us out of the comfort zone of who we think we are and into the great vast opening of urges.

A landscape littered with the bodies of everyone who didn't get it right. Emotionally slain people who lacked insight into what fueled their desires. A landscape of limbo and innuendo. We don't talk about how things don't fit. Culturally the language we use is one that addresses how to change. Twist it, cram it, shove it. Stick it in the freaking hole and hold it there. And we wonder why sex is so deeply unfulfilling. That last thought was so deeply unfulfilling that I stopped. My fingers spread as I flattened the book open in my hand.

Erotic Book Night was in a few days. It was my turn to host. We could have met at someone else's apartment but ultimately I was lazy and offered. I am a lazy perfectionist. Hosting meant I didn't have to leave my apartment.

Lazy or not, I still had those panties.

ii.

The feeling started out in the kitchen. Odd, out of place, squeezed in-between a vintage sugar canister and the knife block. So it moved to the coffee table in the living room next to four Arabian Night scented pillar candles from the after Christmas sale my cheap ass rationed by only lighting for special occasions. I.e., Never. I had a lot of space. Since the boyfriend had moved out I'd cleaned but not rearranged. Caleb was a packrat and a hipster douche bag sports enthusiast. For two years every available space was filled with helmets, canoes, paddles, knee pads. Now I could stretch out in my space and admire my feeling.

After a few glasses of Concha el Toro the feeling commanded more of my attention. Studying the angles, I convinced myself it was a heart. Valves jutted up from the open center. A bumpy, lumpy, puke green heart.

It remained a quiet side piece until my downstairs neighbor Ramon broke up with his girlfriend. El Jimador Blanco bottle in hand he appeared at my door at 12:17 AM still glued to and obsessing over his phone. "When will she ever stop texting me?"

I shrugged. The mystery of life.

I did not have an answer for that question.

I did have three fresh limes and salt.

What started as a charade in macho ambivalence quickly descended into weep fest.

"I loved her," he stammered, his soft Latin accent pronouncing it, "Eye wuvvv her."

"I know you did," I said.

Lick it. Slam it. Suck it.

Tears streamed down his chubby cheeks.

The thing is that you can't date up. You can only date to your speed or date down, which is less preferable, but you cannot date up. It is a long, tedious nightmare. And Christy was up. Unfortunately. She was smarter than him, prettier than him and the attention she got from other guys made him a bona fide lunatic.

So she yelled at him.

In public.

And they broke up.

The end.

Not really.

My phone rang. I ignored it. Most people snatched up the phone after midnight. Not me. Single people with disposable income and their own apartment never benefited from midnight callers. Those callers needed money, rides, couches, moral support. None of which I offered. The call went to voice mail. I ignored it because Ramon was enough to deal with until the caller rang back five times in a row. I glared at the unfamiliar number on my screen, set up another row of shots for grieving Ramon and excused myself.

I dialed the number.

"Hello," Eloise whispered.

"Where are you?"

"In a Motel 6."

"Whose phone are you calling from?"

"I had to disconnect my phone. I'm using one of those prepaid ones from Wal-Mart."

What I wanted to say was, "You're staying in a Motel 6 and you set foot in a Wal-Mart?"

Instead I asked, "Are you okay?" because clearly she wasn't. My nose twitched. I leaned back, glancing through the doorway into the living room. Ramon had fired up a Lucky Strike.

"I'm sort of underground," Eloise said.

"Ummm, what does that mean?"

"It means that John was really mad when he got back from Palm Springs and found out about the yard sale."

Oh. *That.*

Tequila whirred in my bloodstream. "What are you going to do?" I peeled the paper wrapping off of a blueberry muffin and snarfed it down, trying to maintain a buzz and not go straight to drunk.

"I'm gonna file this time. I'm done."

"That was kind of obvious when you sold his golf clubs. Where are you?"

"I'm going to Flagstaff. I just have to finalize a few things. How's the feeling?"

I swallowed. Dry muffin turned my mouth into a desert. I glanced back into the living room. Ramon lay sprawled on the couch, flicking ashes into the center of the feeling. A burning ember, ashes, and smoke inside a lumpy heart. Ramon took a swig of tequila.

"It's good," I said. "Practical. A centerpiece. It's getting a fair amount of attention."

"Good," she said firmly. "I put a piece of my soul into creating that piece of art."

The same one currently being filled with cigarette butts.

"Take care of it," she sighed. "I'll call you when I get to Arizona. You can visit."

"Sounds like a plan."

She sighed big and loud. "Plans suck."

I walked into the living room. Smoke twirled up and around Ramon's face, his dark eyes heady and languid. I thought he was about to say something interesting, instead he leaned back, made eye contact and said, "That is the ugliest ashtray I've ever seen. It makes me want to cry."

4:14 AM.

A heart full of ashes.

Ramon stumbled drunk and weary into the hall, promising to return. I emptied the feeling, washed the inside of the lumpy heart, negating intense guilt. I had a buzz. Ramon was grieving the end of his two month, twenty four day, earth shattering love affair. Insomnia arrived without notice. Me and the feeling watched reruns of Gilligan's Island. A ridiculous show but my father had loved it. The Professor was his favorite character. I had fond memories of him sitting up late at night at the island stove, finishing up his notes and laughing in that gentle way people do when they are genuinely amused. I wondered if the feeling could be a kind of oracle, a crystal ball. Like I could lay my hands on it and divine the future. Grab its strange valves, jutting out from the center and beg for holy, righteous guidance.

iii.

Erotic Book Night. EBN to us seasoned pros. It was my night to host. Since there was now an ashtray on the end table everyone assumed they could fire up. I opened the window to the fire escape and left it at that, too tired to argue.

Kate read passages of erotic fairy tales aloud as she flicked Camel filter ashes into the feeling.

I watched, mesmerized by the sight of a smoking heart. A heart on fire.

Okay.

Maybe it was the wine.

Red I can handle.

White makes me sway like a drunk stripper.

"I love it when you dance us to the door," Erin cooed.

I decided right then all wine makers should make people video tape themselves from cork pop to passing out.

Though no one has ever passed out on wine.

Technically.

Because wine is more like an art form with the aging, tasting, breathing.

Less like alcohol.

It's like a coincidence that wine is even alcoholic.

So I was on that thought, looking down at my yellow rubber gloves, cleaning out the crevices of a violated heart.

A heart on fire.

Smoking.

A heart not merely content to be a non-specific, generic, broad feeling.

Obsessing meant I was hungry. Low blood sugar created a nasty loop in my brain. I set the feeling upside down in the drain and popped off my rubber gloves.

Three Fortune Cookies sat on the counter in front of me. I closed my eyes and mixed them all up, choosing one quick. I cracked open the oracle. And read.

It was blank.

Argh.

Of all the times for a fortune cookie to malfunction.

I needed a sign from the universe.

A nudge from destiny.

A bright, flashing sign.

Anything.

To let me know I was on task, on track, purposeful.

Work as I knew it was copyediting for a company that owned five magazines, three of which were related to the great outdoors. {Shrug}. What could I say. I was great at copy regarding fishing and Moose tracking. I was also the only vegetarian in an office full of men I would never date. Flannel and Fleece, I called them, though not to their bearded faces. Beards are for dragons, Erin liked to say.

I was halfway through an article about how to avoid forest fires when I suddenly wondered what the feeling was doing.

It was upside down.

Damp, possibly dry.

In a semi unfamiliar place.

A metaphor for me.

If I liked metaphors.

Which I didn't.

I avoided the feeling.

Eloise called to say she'd met a man at a honky tonk.

"Pardon me for saying this, but have you gone crazy?"

"It was the only place open and I was hungry," she said cryptically.

This from the woman who sends her salad back to the kitchen when the lettuce is too dry.

"Where are you?"

"Oklahoma."

"Does he have all of his teeth?"

"Don't be rude."

Her goodbye was curt but I could tell she secretly admired my sarcasm.

I went back to cleaning and sorting my walk-in. Pants. Shirts. Short sleeves. Tees. Straps. Larger questions loomed on the horizon like what was I gonna be when I grow up.

Which was about ten years ago.

By my calculations.

Twelve by normal standards.

I was having a hard time making grown up decisions. So I threw my money away renting and getting facials. It was why I loved my building so much. None of us had bought into the whole grown up thing.

I took a break to get a Ginger Ale. The feeling watched me from the end table. The small table made it look larger. Like it was expanding.

Erin buzzed the doorbell at 6:14 and saved me from existential hell.

"I thought you were going out for Long Island Iced Teas with that chick from work." I closed the front door and watched Erin teeter down the hall to the kitchen.

I snuck a glance at the feeling.

It looked shiny but docile.

Erin was half stuffed into the refrigerator eating hummus and leftover lentil loaf with a wooden serving fork she found on the counter.

"I did," she said, mouth full, making it sound like "I whid."

"So what are you doing here?"

"She kept asking me if I liked to do dance parties in my bedroom."

"Do you?" Flat Ginger Ale burned my tongue.

"No. I don't. But that wasn't what bothered me."

"Are you going to tell me or do you want me to ask?"

"I'm going to tell you." She flipped open a carton with the curious look of a girl who drank too much alcohol on an empty stomach. "Oh, god. Sesame noodles. You are my savior." Standing upright she shoveled food in her mouth and in-between bites managed to form sentences. "I swear the whole dance party thing was some secret code for let's get it on."

Not what I expected her to say. "Oh. Did she say anything else?"

"Yeah." Erin swallowed her most ambitious bite of cold take out yet. "She told me I had the greatest tits she'd ever seen."

"Awkward."

"To say the least." She pushed off from the counter. "I have to sit down. What are you doing?"

"Avoiding real life by cleaning out my closet."

She cocked an eyebrow. "I don't believe you. You hate cleaning."

She kicked off her shoes and took up residence on the sofa.

I changed the subject. "What was your favorite thing to do on the playground?"

Too weary and drunk to argue she played along. "Monkey bars. I was fucking Queen of the Monkey bars." She ran her index finger down and around the contours of the feeling. "What is this exactly?"

"High art. I bought it from Eloise. She sold everything while John was out of town."

Erin swung around. "What? Hot John is single?"

I rolled my eyes.

"Don't act like he hasn't flirted with you at every holiday party since they married."

"They're better off divorced," I said cryptically because observations like that unnerved me.

"Good for her. How is she?"

"She is seeing a man that she met in a honky tonk who may or may not have teeth."

Erin cocked that eyebrow. "Sounds complicated."

The doorbell rang.

Erin licked the serving fork she'd held onto and set it on top of the carton. "If we get enough people we can have a dance party."

Ramon was standing in the hallway when I opened my door.

Hot Christy struck again.

"Hearts deserve more time," Erin said, uncharacteristically poignant as she slung her legs over the coffee table and draped her arm over the side of the sofa, precariously close to the feeling.

Ramon's face pinched tight as he crumpled into a chair. "Christy stole Fang Goya. She is an evil bitch."

Landmark moment.

Erin and I looked at each other. Instinctively she reached for the feeling. Her fingertips tapped the swooping curves.

Ramon wailed. "Fang Goya."

I shrugged. "Email me a photo. I'll start making flyers."

"Did you check the basement. He has gone down the garbage shoot a few times on his on," Erin offered.

iv.

Things no one talks about.

Squiggly little naked stick figures screwing.

Dirty but justified in the name of art. Strangely erotic. Perfect for EBN. Line drawings of thighs and boobs, naked white spaces, normally filled with ink or flesh or clothes, now bare. The blank spaceness of it all suggested nudity. Filling in the blanks kept society in check. The poetic thigh resting against a bare chest, tells a tale of surrender.

A tale of secrets.

That's what feelings really are.

Secrets.

Because no one can ever know the full extent of what we feel. The parts no one ever gets to see. The parts that make us an island. Float on. Drift out. Erotic is a kind of window looking into the person you want to be on top of. Intimacy is overrated.

Sex is never something to take seriously. Nudity, grace and vulnerability only come at the hands of strangers.

I'd rather be an object of desire.

I thought about the feeling. I'd moved it to the window ledge by the plants. Perhaps it was a chaste feeling. Not given to particular appetites.

I pulled my college panties out of the back of the drawer and slipped them up and over my thighs.

v.

Traffic surged through the streets, a swell of steel moving forward and back. Rumbling, honking. The sound of tires slapping wet streets. That long *streeeeeeck* sound that water molecules make when disbursed. I was fiddling with my umbrella when it suddenly opened in a man's face.

I stepped back a little horrified. He touched his nose and chin, checking for blood, then looked straight at me.

John.

Dark hair trimmed neat, flecks of gray. The most stunning blue gray eyes you've ever seen. Tall, broad shoulders and chest. These big hands I'd always wanted to feel all over my body.

Even when he was with Eloise.

Which he wasn't.

And that opened up a whole new set of options.

"Cora?"

"John."

He stepped back in the rain, looking me up and down. "How are you?"

"Good," I shrugged. "You?"

I braced myself for the spew of profanity about to come out of his mouth beginning with, "She sold my fucking golf clubs. Who sells a man's golf clubs?"

"Okay," he said convincingly which disturbed me more than profanity.

Because I'd expected a different answer, I stared blankly at him until he pointed at the small bag in my hand.

"A gift?"

"A book," I said, handing it over.

Carefully he slid the book from the bag and stared at the cover.

The erotic poetry and drawings of e.e. cummings.

Careful not to get it wet, he fingered the pages lightly. "I was just going around the corner to have a glass of wine. Why don't you join me? We'll catch up. It's been, what? Half a year since we saw each other?"

Wine was tempting. The disheveled boyishness of John was amplified by the way he handed my book back and shoved his hands in his pockets, waiting.

Two glasses of Pinot Noir and one Beaujolais-Village later and we were back in my apartment. A cool humid air hung in the hall. The lights were out. My hand reached for the switch. I felt John's hand slide up my belly to my breasts. I'd offered to make us a quick dinner. Quesadillas with goat cheese and fresh jalapenos. A ludicrous idea fueled by wine that insisted I impress this man with my culinary skills.

Except that man was my best friend's soon to be ex-husband.

And he was pulling my panties down with one hand.

But those hands felt so good on my body. How they slid effortlessly across my skin.

"I've wanted you for a long time, Cora," he said quietly in the dark.

The completely shallow words every girl wants to hear.

I want you.

Now.

In the hall. Right here on the Ikea rug.

There was a moment tumbling to the floor where I questioned the moral dilemma of what I was about to do. But "Ex" was the key word here. The game changer. The decider. Eloise was off making out with some guy in a honky tonk.

John was now a free zone.

A hot free zone.

Back on the market after eight years.

So there I was on top, straddling him in the moonlight, my thighs squeezing him tight, the blissful intoxication of his mouth on mine. The feeling of his chest under my fingertips.

"Are you taking anything?" he whispered.

"From who," I responded, dazed by the question.

My hips moved in time to my heartbeat.

"Birth control pills? Condoms? I don't have anything on me."

"I'm on you," I said in the most sarcastic tone I'd ever heard myself use. We'd reached the grown up portion of our interlude. The part where he suddenly reminded me that we should have talked about this before finding ourselves half naked on the floor.

"No," I answered truthfully.

And because of this answer, when the time came, he hoisted me into the air and held me there to finish up.

Awkward and sudden.

We laid together quietly on the rug. I pulled a trench coat down from the rack to cover us in the damp chill.

"That was exceptionally good," John mused.

I smiled. Mmm-hmmm. Good.

Bang. Bang. Bang.

A breath caught in my throat. John laid his hand on my thigh.

I prayed silently that the visitor would go away.

"Cora. Cora. Opens ze door. Fang Goya has returned home to papi."

Ramon.

In a single blinding millisecond, I knew exactly what was about to happen.

Hall light spilled over our bodies. John shielded his eyes, looking up, making a disgruntled noise.

Ramon took exactly three steps inside, looked down and gasped. "Are you injured?"

In his arms, he held the ugliest cat to ever manifest on planet Earth. Severely obese, tongue hanging out, a huge fang on the left side of his mouth, made more pronounced by the fact that the right tooth was missing, big strange colored stripes glopped all over his body. Ramon had found him in a drainage ditch ten years ago when he was working for a tech company in San Jose.

"Oh," he said, innocently. "I had no idea."

"You would have if you'd knocked," John growled.

His hand was still on my thigh but didn't feel sweet and tender anymore.

Ramon backed away like he'd witnessed a crime. "Perhaps, later we will talk."

"I'll come over in a little awhile."

The door clicked shut.

Both of us laid silent on the rug.

Finally, John raised up on an elbow, kissed my nose and said, "I have to get home."

In an effort to make small talk that didn't seem like I was dredging up his broken marriage, I asked, "Are you going to sell the house?"

He slipped effortlessly into his trousers, perfectly balanced. "Why would I do that?"

I shrugged, suddenly unsure of my need to conceal the real motive for asking. "Because."

He frowned so intensely I could see the corners of his lips pinched, even in the dim streetlight from the living room windows. "I'm not selling the house. Eloise will just have to learn to deal with it."

"Oh." I stood and pulled my skirt down to cover my knees.

"I'll tell her you said, 'hi'. Where's your bathroom?"

"Through the living room," I pointed. "That way." Then the slow, insidious reality of what he'd just said hit me and I asked, "When?"

John zipped his pants and smoothed the wrinkles out. "When what?" Lightly brushing his lips against mine, he added, "When can we do this again?"

I backed into the coat rack. "No. When are you going to tell her I said, 'hi'?"

"Tonight."

"When she calls?"

John cocked his head to the side and his hair tumbled down over his forehead. "Why would she call? She's at home."

"What home?"

Stepping back, he looked me up and down. "Cora, are you okay?"

"Where's Eloise?" I asked. My voice rose high and shrill.

Very slowly, careful to enunciate every letter, he said, "I told you she's at home."

I swallowed. "I thought she left."

He laughed, shook his head and sighed in a way that said none of it was funny. "She took this ridiculous trip out west to the desert but she's home now. I'll tell her to call you."

"But she..."

He stepped into the living room, pausing to stare at the feeling, silhouetted in the fading twilight. He cocked his head to the other side. "Where did you get that?"

"Eloise. It was— she gave it to me."

"You know she made that for me? For our anniversary."

A seething, dark pit opened in my stomach, threatening to suck me inside forever.

I smiled, as fake as ever, and said, "No. As a matter of fact, I did not know that."

"Humpf," he mused. Then walked through the dark living room into the even darker hall and disappeared.

Something unholy and angry swelled within me. I briefly considered the fact that he could be lying. He could be playing it off to get information. To get me to reveal her whereabouts. Without making a sound, I tiptoed to the kitchen and picked up my phone. In the strange early evening darkness I pressed the autodial for Eloise's home number. With my other ear I listened to make sure John wasn't sneaking up on me. Three rings. Four rings. A deep relief spread from my chest outward.

John was lying.

Trying to get me to give up details only I would know.

Seven rings.

My thumb slid across the keypad to end the call.

"Hello?"

My breath choked in my throat.

"Hello?" Eloise said again on the other end of the line.

She sounded groggy, tired.

Without thinking my thumb pressed the button and ended the call.

I stood there trying to rid myself of a creeping panic.

The front door closed quietly. I stepped around the corner. The rooms were empty. Immediately my eyes turned to the feeling, ready to rescue it from John's possessive glare.

And it was gone.

A big empty space in-between the plants.

My hands started to tremble. Not only had he left without saying goodbye, he'd stolen my feeling. Taken it without asking. Insinuated his way into my bed. If my bed were in the hallway.

What a bastard.

My phone rang in my hand. I didn't have to look down to know Eloise's name was flashing on the screen. I had no idea what to say. I tossed my phone on the sofa and went to find my keys. For a split second I considered running after John. He couldn't just take something from me without asking. But that deep, angry panic rose again and I knew the answer.

Let him have it.

It was always his.

Some feelings just aren't worth holding onto.

Twelve Drawers

A dresser was crammed in the corner, under a thick layer of dust. It had twelve drawers. Each one was a trip into the past. It's where I found the pictures of my Mother with the man. They were young, she in a black velvet mini dress, brown hair tumbling down over her shoulders. He looked normal. That was the first clue. I was sure I'd never seen him before. When I smelled biscuits cooking I stopped with the detective work and went downstairs.

I told my grandmother, "I know my mother was with someone before my dad. I saw him."

That got her attention. She turned from the iron skillet where she was tossing carrots and potatoes. "What?" she asked cautiously.

"I know there was someone else."

For a long time she stood very still, staring at the broken clock on the stove. Then her eyes trailed up to the grease stains on the wall. When her fingers found the carrots again, her mouth found words.

"Well, it might be time to tell you that the person you think is your father isn't really your father."

The words clobbered me. I wanted to pretend like it didn't matter, like I already knew, so I pulled open the oven door. The hot, dry air slammed into my face, drying my eyes. I looked closer. The light bulb was blown. Dough was rising.

"Are you okay?" she asked. "I'm not trying to surprise you but your mother will never tell you this so I might as well. There's no sense in you spending your entire life stuck down in her pack of lies."

Then she told me. Told me how my mother had run off to North Carolina with a boy still in high school and lived at his house with his mother and three brothers. She told me how he'd come to live here, in this house, in the room with the dresser and it's twelve drawers. She talked about his sweet face and blond hair...

"Blond hair," I interrupted. "He doesn't have blond hair."

"Who?"

"The man in the pictures."

"What pictures?" She asked slowly, sure she'd said too much.

The sun was setting. It was July. Outside, the streetlights clicked on. Dinner would be late tonight.

86 Miles from El Paso

Anna Strong is thin and dry and smells like dust. One night she drives from the arms of the devil through an Alabama night, down into the ache of Mississippi, passing through Parishes. When exhaustion closes her eyes she is laying on a lumpy pillow in Louisiana. Dreams come differently now. They come with snake rattlers and oil wells. The desert warm winter glides past this place where Indians and batteries lay smashed underfoot in the street. Empty packages of buffalo jerky line the floorboards. The red car drives past lizards, sunning on rocks, to the Rio Grande. Past the subservient oil wells that fuck the earth for petroleum. The unforgiven sheds itself in this place, America, leaving its skin to dry with scorpion shells. Roadside naps sedate her all rolled up with her knees on either side of the steering wheel. Then there are the missions, hunkered low in the heat, saving souls. 86 miles from El Paso she hikes high into the mountain dwellings of people who left a thousand years ago. They do not know her but she knows them. What is left of their life is in a broken pot at the edge of a precipice. The fire that burned the rock ceiling knows her hand now. Something drove these people high. The same fire drives her into a burning ceremony of herself. Buttons of peyote help her connect the dots. She vomits into the stream while the shaman shakes a rattle behind her head so that her soul does not escape. Dark shadows push the moon high. Decrepit pots hold water she swishes around in her mouth, refusing to swallow. The rocks watch her sleep all night. With dawn she inches away from the edge with breath that is slim, formed by becoming.

Coming down from the mountain she descends into the path of the ancestors, full stride, blowing through El Capitan. It is the nuance of nothingness that holds her captive in this place with its spiky, predatory stillness. The next morning a dust storm blows through El Paso and she closes the windows, haunted. In the stirring swirl of dusty fortitude she rides a cowboy well into the night. It is his horse she wants to rustle from the front yard to ride out with the wolves. The city disappears into the howling, violent sand. At 4 AM a chilled air is ascending. There are cowboy boots on the floor. She pours a glass of water, naked, staring out across the border. The sound of the faucet stutters. There are old blankets and sadness all over the floor.

Plastic

Our love was plastic. Gas station, checkout counter, plastic.
Glossy.
Slippery.
Stick on.
Scratch and sniff.
Sometimes stories just start in mid-sentence. Ours did. And it's hard to catch your breath.

We were a box of red hots melting on the dash of a Chevy. Our love had a little dust on it dangling from the rearview mirror, creases in the fold because we took it in and out too much. Hot cherry scented breath transported me back to the hallway in Junior High. I giggled, tempted by the fate of sighs and thighs. The tattoo of a Thunderbird stretched across his back. Sweet, honey breath tickled my hair. Brightly painted red nails reflected sunlight.

It was Sunday. Respectful people were praying. I was the only unmarried person in the room. Remote control, ice bucket, and little plastic cups became the holy items of our sacrifice. Caught in-between the edges of lives that only fit us sometimes, we hurled ourselves head long into the middle of a South Carolina winter.

It snowed that year. Piles of powdery snow clung to Palmetto trees. Held captive by weather in a mirrored motel room, rich with the thick scent of Mongolian beef. The paper menu said he was born the year of the snake. I believe that now. So does his wife. We'd burned so hot for so long.

Plastic always melts.

Dirty Nickel

Tie a cherry stem with your tongue. Copious amounts of alcohol are required. Do it in a bar in St. Louis. Act like you have something to prove. Tie it with your tongue. Then stumble back to your overpriced fourth floor walkup in the Central West End. It's actually your boyfriend's apartment. You would have mentioned that first if you weren't drunk. He's lost something of yours, thrown it away, carelessly. He's not really into consequences or *things*. Pick a fight. A good one. Fight nasty. Fight to the death. Not really. But seriously, get personal. Scream so loud that the fat chicks in Pharmacy school downstairs complain. Leave. Stomp your drunk ass to the bottom of the stairs, out into an autumn night with no shoes or coat. It's 3:23 AM. In the parking lot you see a dirty nickel on the ground. Tarnished, flat on one side. Dirty or not, put it in your pocket.

You will begin to think you are destined for great things.

Walk to the all-night diner. A guy in a booth clears his throat, offers to take you anywhere. Let him drive you across town to your dorm. Walk up the back stairwell. He walks with you because it's dark and scary and while he may be a stranger he is still a gentleman. You, on the other hand, are drunk and need that shoulder to lean on. Thank him at your door. Then throw up in your suitemate's bathroom. Lay down with a wretched, vile taste in your mouth and spin. Think about cherries. The kind in the jar. Stare at the ceiling, floating in a sweet, sugar syrup. Think of the stranger. Imagine him there. Imagine how you could tie his stem with your tongue.

Wake five hours later still wearing your clothes. Roommate pacing, rehearsing lines to Hamlet. Tell her to shut up. Pull a pillow over your head. Wonder when you became such a bitch.

Go to class. Literature. Classics. Feel good about yourself. At least you can read. The lesson is The Love Song of Alfred J. Prufrock. You do not understand this poem. Do not understand why the women come and go. You are looking forward to The Last Temptation of Christ. Contemplate temptation. What it really means. Sneak pieces of dry toast out of your pocket and into your mouth. Go ahead. It's wrapped in a napkin in your pocket. Goggle the definition for temptation on your phone.

temp·ta·tion (noun) To induce or entice, to be inviting, to incline strongly.

You've got that shit on a leash.

Pay attention. Your professor is hot. Go to his office after class and smoke cigarettes. Pray he makes some totally inappropriate move. He won't. Think about how one Tom Collins might level your hangover out. Walk back to your dorm. Think about your life. Create a list of goals. Forget 87% of them by the time you reach the stairs.

You don't need goals because you have a motto. A functional one. Enough vodka explains everything.

Walk down the quiet, carpeted hall. The stranger from last night leans against your door, reading a book. Motorcycle boots, jeans. Notice how hot he is. Wonder why you didn't notice last night. Accept that drunkenness impairs vision. Accept that you don't remember much about last night.
Wait for him to look up.
He will. When he does, *melt*.
Like butter.
Surrender. You are a rowboat going over a waterfall.
Go with it.

He will close his book, hold his place with an index finger, tell you he came to check on you, was worried because you were barefoot and drunk and crying.

You won't remember the crying. Keep that part to yourself.

Instead be polite, engaging, say hello, curtsey, laugh in that little girl way that makes grown men stupid.

Invite him in.

He will politely decline.

Bargain with gods you've never believed in for a kiss.

Just one.

A single, long, dazzling kiss.

Admit you aren't paying attention and ask him to repeat what he just said.

He will quietly, confidently ask you on a road trip.

Entertain the thought that he's a total psycho. Maybe a perv.

But something in those blue, gray eyes tells a deeper truth than can be spoken aloud.

Remember the lines from class. Let us go then, you and I, when the evening is spread out against the sky. Indeed there will be time to wonder, "Do I dare?" and, "Do I dare?"

Time to turn back and descend the stair.

Descend that back stairwell with a mysterious stranger.

You won't even know his name. This will occur to you in the front seat of his gas guzzling 68 royal blue Mustang. Point out that you haven't been properly introduced. The stranger will inform you that you won't be exchanging names. Somewhere during the journey you will form a new name, based on experience. You will think this weird, but kinda hot.

The Mustang speeds down the ramp to the highway.

Break up with your boyfriend in a text. Tell him you know he fucked the server at Bennigan's in May. It won't break his heart. He hasn't even called. The ride to the state line will be strange. Silence will unfold in a trickling sensation. Feel your way through mile markers. Like walking across a dark room, too terrified and excited to touch anything. Wonder what you are doing. A cool breeze blows mercilessly through your hair. Watch the Stranger grip the steering wheel, note how his thighs flex pressing the gas pedal. You pray, really pray for the first time in your life that you are not dreaming. The sound of the highway is a lullaby. Your head drifts to the window. Evaporated vodka pounds inside your skull.

Wake in the parking lot of a steakhouse. It's dark now. The Stranger is outside the car pacing, smoking, talking on his phone. Groan, wipe drool from your cheek. Make mental note not to get plastered. Follow up Dr. Phil moment with realization that alcoholism may be in your future. Accept genetic coding. Rum Daddy. Gin Mommy.

You don't know it yet but you are at the Kansas border.

With a guy you don't know. Who looks over and sees that you're awake. He hangs up his phone quickly. Not like he's been caught but like he's been waiting. You hope he didn't pay for his very expensive, fully restored Mustang by dealing in human trafficking. Notice that you forgot to shower. Open the car door, step into a cool night. Feel the air on your cheek. Really feel it. It's blown across the world just to graze your skin. It's on its way across the plains now, to the East Coast where it will leave land and launch across the Atlantic and blow through the Strait of Gibraltar. The same wind circles the planet. Charged particles crackle across the landscape. The wind is alive.

One long loop. Same as your life.

This is what happens with less drinking and more thinking.

Hold your arms out wide.

So wide.

Stretch.
Spin out into the world.
Go ahead.
The Stranger will think you are a bohemian.
You smell like a truck driver.

The restaurant air is thick with steak and baked potatoes. Your mouth will water. Excuse yourself to the Little Girls Room. Think about the absurdity of that name. A room for little girls. Go directly to the mirror. Expect the worst. Be pleasantly surprised. Hair tousled. Skin glowing. Eyes a little brighter. Clothes wrinkled.

Sit across the table. Watch how the Stranger talks to you, listens to you, how the candlelight flickers across his face and neck. Take your first bite of steak. Feel it melt in your mouth. Close your eyes, moan. Promise to eat salad later.

Ask the Stranger what he was doing at the diner when you stumbled in drunk last night after fighting with your boyfriend.

Ex-boyfriend.

He will tell you his friend works the graveyard shift.

Ask where you are going.

Montana, he says. Then Portland. I have friends we can stay with.

Wonder what the fuck you are doing.

Briefly.

Don't linger in doubt but definitely entertain the thought.

Ask him why he's doing this.

He will say you look like a girl who needs to get away.

Contemplate this.

Contemplate how nice it is to be in the middle of the United States with a total stranger who is hot and doesn't seem psycho. Contemplate how easy it was to drive away from all of those things you thought you could never live without.

The Stranger asks where you are from.

Tell him about growing up in Mississippi. About levees and sunsets and rivers that flow.

Flow with it. Let the conversation come easy.

Don't try to impress. Not once. Not even a little.

Don't talk about daddy's run in the House of Representatives or how mama runs the Literacy Project.

Talk about you.

Because he asks what you want out of life.

Ask the Stranger what he does in his spare time. He will tell you he owns a shipping business. It's the off season. More time to explore.

Leave the steakhouse high on conversation and food and hot guy mojo. Listen to the gravel crunch under your Keds. Wonder how many more years you can put off declaring your major. With parental financial contributions it could go on indefinitely.

The Stranger opens the car door.

Pause to remember the last time a man opened a door for you.

Something deep and unidentifiable inside you begins to howl. An indescribable anguish.

Let it howl.

Let it disturb you.

Shiver in the cold.

Something inside of you breaks loose. A cold, stillness permeates the lining of your skin. A low howl churns in the bottom of your gut.

The Stranger lays his hand on your shoulder, asks if you are okay.

You think of vodka but pour steaming black coffee into a cup at a gas station.

The next few hours will lead you into South Dakota.

You offer to drive.

The Stranger rips open little sugar packets with his teeth and pours them into his cup.

Tells you he's got it.

Pull your legs up girlishly beneath you on the front seat and talk about childhood foods.

Egg salad.

Fried corn.

Coke floats.

Ask him where he's from.

He tells you Alabama via upstate New York.

Drive deep into the night, trading stories, listening to Indian radio stations and the soundtrack to Magnolia on repeat.

Your roommate sends a text.

Ignore. Delete.

You are now certain that in the last precious seconds of your life, bad roommates will not flash before your eyes.

It's not until you check into a roadside motel at 6:43 AM that you really start wondering.

What's going on?

I mean, you're about to fall asleep in a motel room with a strange guy you've driven over five hundred miles with in one day.

He's not your friend. Per se. Definitely not a booty call.

There's zero alcohol involved.

Exhausted and confused you flop back on a double bed and wait for him to make a move. You're wearing jeans but open your legs invitingly, let your arms fall to your sides, sigh.

Think about cherries. The kind in the jar. Stare at the ceiling and think about floating in a sweet, sugar syrup. Think of the stranger. Imagine him there. Floating with you.

Will it be worth it, after all, will it be worthwhile, after the sunsets and the dooryards and the sprinkled streets, will it be worth it to float with him.

Wake midafternoon to the sounds of housekeeping in the hall.

Purse on nightstand. Jeans untouched.

Neither psycho, nor perv.

Contemplate how you feel about that since you were counting on one or the other.

Sit up in bed.

No ruthless hangover slams into you.

Your mouth is furry and dry.

The aching realization that something is horribly wrong with your life descends.

The howl returns.

It rips at screaming Christmas memories. The howl is bigger than you so you don't fight back. You pull your weird, scratchy motel binky over your head and cry.

The Stranger finds you this way.

This time last year you never would have imagined yourself in a motel in South Dakota with some guy from a diner.

You don't miss your boyfriend.

Not even a little.

You are free.

Free from what bound you.

You traded it for the howl.

The Stranger will hand you a cup of coffee, ask if you're okay.

You nod.

He won't believe you.

You won't believe you.

But you've been lying about the delusions of your life for so long that you're not giving up that easy.

You may go insane but you'll be dragged.

This crack up brings a disturbing superpower. You start to see people as they are and not as you want them to be. This will have its drawbacks.

You form a plan in the motel. You and the Stranger. You will shop at Thrift stores and pick out clothes for each other.

Beginning now.

Each will create an identity for the other.

St. Vincent's Thrift Store. The Stranger chooses a pink, fuzzy jacket and purple velvet pants. You stare at him, wondering why he's dressing you like a Florida divorcee.

Nothing makes sense.

Go with it.

Do you dare? Do you dare?

From a back rack choose a sweet, dark chocolate, pink pin striped suit that appeals to your cinematic side. You're not sure he can pull it off.

Allow yourself to be pleasantly surprised when he steps out of the dressing room rocking the suit with a white, open collar, button down shirt and motorcycle boots.

Melt a little.

Quiver at the sight.

You know you want to.

Pinch your face up in that weird way people do when they are about to squee with joy.

At your suggestion the Stranger will choose a pale pink camisole to complete your outfit.

It's cheating but it hardly matters. Since you're making it up.

The dressing room will smell like Pine Sol scented mothballs. Change into a cami that looks sexy with purple velvet pants. Catch a glimpse of the Strangers face when you step into the short hall. Notice how his face softens. You've never seen that look on a man's face before. Maybe in movies. Never in real life.

In the back of a thrift store in Sioux Falls watch the Stranger look you up and down. Get a little drunk off of that feeling. Especially when you tell him you need a handbag and he chooses a 1950's Lucite purse with a pink heart clasp. Without anyone noticing, you will slide that dirty nickel down into the pocket of your new pants.

Across a landscape of cornfields, wheat fields, fields of fields. Under the watchful gaze of sometimes sunshine. Under the sweet blaze of winter coming. A murmur of insects. Words cascade down to your lips where you suck them in like a wild song from the bayou. Remember driving through parishes at night to your grandmother's house. Through a childhood. Let the wide-open landscape rise within you. You want to lie down in sweet grass next to the ants, grasshoppers, dragonflies whizzing.

All new.

All enticing.

A wide-open paradise of dust and sky.

Front seat conversation will go something like this.

You will now know all about his shipping company. How he created the model in college for a class.

He owns a Ducati.

Has an older brother who is a Preacher.

A guitar he never plays.

A messy office.

A telescope for spying on neighbors.

On a highway. 1 AM. Jacked on caffeine. The perfect place to fall in love.

Freudian slip.

The perfect place to get to know someone.

Except you're only throwing pieces.

Parts of the whole.

It takes that dead body on the side of the road to rewind you.

Back to the beginning.

That sounds so dramatic.

Body.

Two lane highway. Man on the ground next to the open door of his Ford Taurus.

The Stranger will pull onto the dirt shoulder, throw on his flashers. From the glove compartment he pulls a gun. You have no idea what kind. He cocks it. This could be an ambush, he whispers.

You lock the passenger's door. Go on hyper alert. Paranoid even.

In the headlights the Stranger kneels next to the body. You will expect it to bolt upright.

The body won't move.

The Stranger yells for you to call 911. Find your phone. Which will of course have no charge. Jump out of the car and run to the hood. The Stranger pumps the guys chest.

Come get my phone out of my pocket, he will yell.

You slide your hand into the pocket of those dark chocolate, pin striped pants and feel around until your fingers grasp the phone and pull it out.

Dial.

Dogs howl in the distance.

Maybe wolves.

911. State your emergency.

Side of the road. Man on highway. Body.

State your location.

Look around. Black fields roll away. Full moon. You have no idea where you are.

An eighteen-wheeler will slow to a stop further down the road. The Trucker runs, change jingling in his pockets.

You reach inside your own pocket and grasp that dirty nickel and thank god you are alive.

Emergency lights explode across the plains. Flashing colors against the sky. Close your eyes. Think of all those people who died last year when a bridge collapsed in Minnesota. Imagine driving off that ragged edge, plunging into cold darkness.

You think of that. Yes you do. Out in your pink, fuzzy jacket, shivering.

Clouds pass in front of the moon. You will listen for clues to the future. Ready to record the slightest detail. You are called from the dark night of your sleep. Courage is your beauty balm. Wear it.

There will be tests of skill.

A path to follow.

A cliff or cave.

You will go down to go up.

Your life will be shaped into star dusted cakes.

A cross. A key. A penny. A poem. A series of numbers. A toad. A golden ribbon. Fields of edible flowers.

Touch the dirty nickel in your pocket.

Your bank account is empty. Not empty. It has seventy-six cents. With the nickel, you have a whooping eighty-one cents saved.

In your old life you avoided dangerous thoughts. In this life you will doubt the fear. It becomes laughable. A joke. A strap that falls away. One that squeezed your neck since childhood. Sirens wail through the night. You toss your head back, face up, shining into the black, sparkling canvas of sky and let out one long howl.

Breathtaking.

The hallowed ground of your old life rushes away like the sea receding from shore. Back into afternoons that ended before they began. Back to a life that was never truly yours, borrowed glasses of Bacardi and parents acting badly. You burrow deeper into your jacket. Balancing on the edge of trust and grace. Surrender the utter absurdity of doing everything right. There's no manual for life. Under a dark night reach up into the age of abandon and grab onto a slow, creeping insanity that grows like a vine from the very center of the earth. Mile markers are the math of the journey. You remember the first time you got alcohol poisoning. How you drank to have sex because it was too intimate and desperate.

The Stranger will walk out into the field, quietly slip his hand into yours. You turn, watch the emergency workers load the stretcher with the body bag strapped to it into the ambulance. You realize goodbye is the other side of hello.

Lights flash.
Blue and white.
Across open plains.
A black stretch of earth.
Fertile and unplowed.
The police ask for ID's to fill out their report.
Without a thought you will hand yours over.
Avoid thinking about the guy with the heart attack.
Cause your heart can attack you.
It's a wicked design flaw.
The same heart that brings love and joy can strike a person dead.
The one thing most deeply associated with love takes you out.
Sorta like god.
A lightning bolt through the heart.
Sayonara.

You wait, shivering in the night chill.
The officer will tell you that you have to come down to the station.
You will stammer, "Did I do something wrong?"
"You're missing," he says, forcing a smile.
The past few days descend like an avalanche of emotion. You can't go back. Not now. Not after all this. There's nothing back in that old world except to be or not to be.
Suddenly you're angry.
Feel cornered.
Watched.
Any second that lightning bolt will come burning out of the sky for you.
You watched your sister die. That tiny baby born strange and premature. Struggling to breathe, to grab onto a single thread of life and pull. Your parents made you go to the hospital and stare silently at her in the little glass box. She spent her short life on earth in a series of boxes, especially the one lowered into the ground.

She was a tiny baby made of eggshells. Cracked apart. A physical rendering of your parents' marriage. Broken, struggling to breathe. A tiny life beating back the arms of death. Your father named her Amelia Rainn. How could such a tiny breath blow away all of that anguish?

You squeeze that dirty nickel in your pocket and imagine Amelia Rainn dropped it down to earth for you to find. That she knew you'd go on this adventure and need a special talisman. You imagine Amelia Rainn saw the Stranger long before you did.

Squeeze that dirty nickel in your pocket.

Squeeze it hard.

Do you dare? Do you dare?

The station will be quiet. Most of the offices have lights out, doors shut. Coffee brews in a break room down the hall. In the big, open squad room the officer will take you to his desk. Instruct you on the art of dialing. The report lays open.

Missing person.

A metaphor for your life.

Always missing.

Never found.

You recognize the number immediately.

Six rings is all it takes for the ungracious past to descend upon you.

Saved by voice mail.

Leave a message.

Lucky you.

In nervous haste you glance at the Stranger. He isn't ripped or buff but life has given him a nice workout. A phone rings on another desk. The officer picks it up, listens, then hands it over to you.

A cold strike of fear splits straight through your howl. Even with the phone so far from your ear you can hear daddy breathing because he won't give up bacon and Newports. He sounds like he's running a marathon. Like a fat kid chasing the ice cream truck. You were that fat kid once.

He will ask if you're there.

Do you dare? Do you dare?

You stutter, find words, fall into hello.

He wants to know if you're okay.

Tell him you're on a mini vacation.

A what? he will ask.

Tell him you're on a road trip with a complete stranger to figure a few things out.

That's when he will start screaming.

The sound of daddy screaming. So controlled, so loud.

Tell him you're not missing anymore and hang up.

The stranger will look at you, stranger than usual.

You will drive back to the two-lane road that cuts straight through the darkness. The sound of tires thump against pavement.

Up ahead on the right.

Close to where you found the body.

On a piece of earth that rises up from a tree lined meadow.

Under a glowing full moon.

A herd of deer.

White tails flick and twitch.

And one of the most magnificent things you've ever seen.

An albino buck. Snow white antlers and fur. A blazing, white buck on a mound of earth pushed up from another world.

Whoa, the Stranger will say, slowing down.

Something new and wild enters your bloodstream.

You step out into the cold, watch the buck turn and look.

You will burn this memory into your mind.

Burn it.

Burn it.

Feel the stranger next to you, your breath mingling in the air.

He will reach for your hand, loop your fingers into his and wait. The buck will flick his tail and run into the trees with the other deer following.

Part of you will go with him. Part of you returns to the car. Either way both parts have grown wild.

The stranger will drive into dawn. So late now it's early. You will get a room at the motel in the next town. 70's paneling on the wall, old dresser. Scratched table. Two chairs.

Empty your pockets, the stranger says. We're going to talk about last things.

Lost things?

Last things, he will say louder. As in, if these were your final seconds on earth what would be the last things you have on you.

Now you understand. You walked out of your dorm room empty handed. Almost empty handed.

You pull out the dirty nickel.

The sum total of your life.

The stranger empties his pockets.

Swiss Army Knife, guitar pick, wallet, phone, old Henry Rollins spoken word ticket stub.

What made you think of this, you ask. These last things?

The man on the side of the road, he will say. You die with whatever you have on you and then like bandits people come and take it away.

I will build a shrine and put your last things inside, you say.

He will look up at you.

Light bleeds through cracks in the curtains.

The bed is so old. The moment is so new.

It's already tomorrow.

Almost winter.

A full moon.

You ask the stranger if he's ever done anything like this before.
The stranger will shake his head.
Where will it end?
It never ends.
Where will it end?
It never ends.
You and the stranger talk about how life is like drawing without
an eraser. Across the page. Down and around the edges. Up again in
a *wheeee* sort of motion. The first lines you drew were so diligent,
rehearsed. Later a few were dashed off. Then there was simply
scribble. The moment is a sketched line of landscape curving across
the page. Colors so rich you bleed into them. You realize you've
drawn a world of fake smiley faces on everything you've touched.
There are all of these doodles you can't erase. You are someone who
ate her erasers. Chewed them right off like the heads of enemies.

Old women talk in the motel hall. Boys laugh and slam doors in
the parking lot.
Your life is a gift to your ancestors.
De ja vu.
They see you.
You've been here before.
Drawn this before.
You're delirious from lack of sleep.
Come again, the sign at the entrance to heaven reads. Come again.
And you go into this future of projected miracles.
You wonder if you can learn to travel on light. You grow old ...
you grow old ...
you will wear the bottoms of your trousers rolled.

You fall asleep staring at your last things on the bedside table.
Rain comes thundering out of the sky.
In the room the women come and go
talking of Michelangelo.

The sound lulls you into a dream.
You have a dirty nickel.
You can do anything.

You Are Such a Poem

Drunk again, unruly, the smell of scotch and gin thick on your tongue drowning out the smell of honeysuckle in the courtyard where you have been intoxicated for three days straight obsessing over dirty stanzas, your stubbily rhyme, your greasy meter. Words make nuisance of you.

Sunset and evening star and here you are still in your bathrobe missing its belt, haggardly threadbare around the collar. *You are such a poem.* Such a cluster of words down the middle of a page enticing me to read based on the economy of images, neatly placed.

You have been sipping too much metaphor today, if such a thing can be true. All of your oranges are Japanese sunrises, skin the bark of maple trees, days line up in circles of infinity. You are testy, refusing to allow even a single sentence to be constructed until someone makes you a martini, dirty and wet.

Slovenly, you smoke, cuss. You are always unemployed, drinking straight from the box of golden Chablis. You are such a poem. Yet, you are so much of what the world strives to be. We want to know what it's like to be you. Bumming smokes and borrowing money to buy deviled eggs and plastic chaise lounges from the Dollar Bin that you call new chic faux antique.

And yet most days you are just like all of the others, unrequited, broken hearted memories formed on pages in the quiet repose of morning light instructing laymen on the art of feeling. You see, I wanted you to be an Italian Renaissance painter, a big lipped movie star, an abandoned house deep in Alabama or at the very least an underwater volcano. But instead, I got you. A drunk who refuses to go to meetings, will not cooperate with prose, picks fights with biography and constantly scoffs at nonfiction, claiming there isn't such a thing as fiction that is not fiction.

You pee outside, howl at the moon, and scratch in unmentionable places. And yet, I cannot remember a life before you showed up promising to pay rent someday.

It must have been unremarkable. Filled with scheduled mealtimes, stacks of newspapers towering on the floor, fresh bed linens and plastic organizers on my desk. Now the clocks have all been thrown away, newspapers shredded, bed linens are worn as capes and I shudder to consider the fate of those organizers.

So, now when I find you outside drunk, wearing a brown wig and frightfully tight purple underwear, I pull up a new chic faux antique, pour you a dirty, wet, triple olive and offer up my attention in the hopes that if I flirt enough with the edges of your sensibility then you just might pick your teeth and tell me a story.

Abandon

Frost comes to the window but I am warm, naked, in the middle
of a great room with windows all around.
No curtains, only shadows cast against white walls.

No furniture. Just one long hallway that leads to a bed.
I am there.
Outside the trees are turning into old women, reaching with
dying fingers into a darkness that comes earlier, stays later.
So we make love long into the night.
When he is not with me my lover is on the phone.
As he showers I slip into his closet, running my fingertips down
the rows of perfectly crisp hand tailored shirts from Hong Kong. He
catches me, laughs, says I am nosey and should be spanked.
He has no idea.
Pulling a shirt from the plastic covering he slides it over my bare
arms. I wear his clothes more and more. I do not know what it
means. It means I belong to him.
His skin smells of expensive cologne, imported cigarettes,
saffron, sandalwood, surrender. Sometimes, late, drinking tequila,
sucking limes, I lay in his arms spinning into dawn.
He says, "I don't know your last name, have never known it."
Then he laughs when I am silent.
He begs, pleads, shivers.
He is like the moon.
Still I refuse.

In the mornings I sleep buried in the scent of pillow talk. Later, wrapped in a long velvet coat I descend the fire escape. My teeth chatter but my body is warm. He begs me to accept gloves, scarf, hat but I won't. The chill does not penetrate his breath deep in the curves of my neck. A heavy sun rises over the avenues of asphalt but still I only know the tremble, the abandon, the scent of me rising from his season, hungry.

The Day You Find Out Your Uncle Was Gunned Down by Police (non-fiction)

The day you find out your uncle was gunned down by police is a normal day. Normal as it gets. Thursday. Perhaps the day before you were thinking about throwback Thursday photos. Planning what to post. This one. That one. You were definitely thinking about the dream where people kept telling you someone from the dead was trying to make contact. You were definitely thinking about that dream. Which is why you look your uncle up on the internet. With a cup of coffee in hand, no almond milk because you are lactose intolerant and too lazy to drive to Trader Joe's on Wednesday night. Remember, it is Thursday. The day you find out your uncle was gunned down by police.

It wasn't recent. The gunning down. That sucks. In the time passed you moved across the country. From the South to the North. To old battlefields and old wars. Old buildings with bullet holes still lodged in the brick. You picked up coffee in the mornings and drove across the battlefields to the first place that felt like home as an adult. You left a way of life that dominated every breath for years. You left. You walked toward a future. You moved. You married. You moved again.

When you hadn't heard from your uncle in a while you sent emails. He loved emoticons and cute little chain emails. There was no response. That worried you enough to send a simple email. One question. *Are you okay?* No reply.

When you finally have a moment from unpacking and turning in projects and moving and marrying and new schools and jobs and cities, you log in and realize you haven't heard from him in a while. A long while. He has children he loves. He doesn't need you to hover over his life micromanaging what he refers to as his senior moments.

But you are Southern and expect the worst so your internet search goes straight for the obituary. And there it is. His full name printed in the local paper where he lived. *Lived.* Past tense. In a single internet search his tense has changed. He's dead. There was a memorial. A funeral. A body. Suddenly you go from being a person to being a body.

He was older. Almost seventy. It could have been of natural causes. Must have been natural causes. Which sucks. But {shrug} it happens. You do another search to find your cousin's address. You have three of them. You will send one a card. Your families have never been particularly close but you liked them a lot.

When you were little, around nine, your uncle moved to California. You saw him years later when he returned for a visit bringing an AT&T phone system that had a built-in answering machine, a speaker phone, and a hold button that played canned Muzak. It was the coolest fucking thing you'd ever seen.

Except he was rude. He believed you should obey regardless of the request. You threw some rocks at your mailbox and he told you to stop. Except they weren't his rocks or his mailbox and you resented him telling you what to do. So you wait until everyone is gone and fill the sink basin with his shaving cream. A huge, carefully formed mound of splendid, squishy foam. Then you wash it down the drain, as if to say, that is how fast I can get rid of you, answering machine or not.

You don't see him again until five years later. When your grandmother dies. It's a mess. You are the only one who knew she was going to die because you'd been sneaking over to see her even though you were forbidden by your mother who was too high to actually enforce rules. So you weren't exactly in the habit of taking her bad advice. You'd seen your grandmother two weeks earlier and she couldn't get out of bed. You knew she was going to die. Knew she was going to do it on her own terms. And she did. No one ordered an autopsy. No one knows what killed her. No one ever will.

Your uncle arrived from California. Of the three uncles you started out with, you have two left. One disappeared years earlier. Went out to buy malt liquor and cheap cigarettes in an old flannel shirt and never came back. His truck was found on a Texas road, doors open, key in the ignition, engine idling, abandoned. Never seen again.

So now you have two.

You watch the adult family members fight over money. Your uncle is having sex with your mom's best friend. Which normally wouldn't generate much drama except she's married. The absurdity of family makes you pray for it to all be settled and over. Your uncle has a long history of not being able to deal with family and goes back to California.

You understand.

Even applaud him for his unwillingness to suffer through endless days of stupid.

Like stoopid.

The kind of stupid that is stoopid.

You don't know it then but when he boards that plane for California, that's the last time you will ever see him again in person. With your own eyes. The year will be 1988.

But let's get back to Thursday. There's a stack of work to do on your desk.

And your uncle's obituary. Survived by children. Grandchildren. And you try to find your cousin's address. What you find instead is a lawsuit filed by your three cousins against the city and the police department and having too many lawyers as friends you immediately know there is a summary and you scroll

   and scroll

   and scroll

to page six.

And read until your eyes and brain don't believe a word of what is typed on the page. For the first time all day you look away from the screen to a gray Pittsburgh morning unfolding outside the window. It is 10:34 AM. Your uncle is dead. He was killed by police serving a search warrant. You stand up. Get a cup of coffee. Drink some water. Stand in the kitchen. This is hard.

Realize that's why he never returned the emails. Realize there will never be any more emoticons. Realize you have no uncles left because the other one died in 2006 and your mother pretended he was still alive until 2009 so she could keep living in the house for free. Yeah, you're *that* kinda family.

Go back to your desk. Listen to the 911 call he made as the police entered his house. Go ahead. Lose yourself in that irony a moment. Calling the police to come save you from the police. Listen to his last words. It's not every day that a person's last words are preserved this way. The final minutes of his life play out. Realize that a TACT team came to his house to execute a search warrant. Go ahead. Luxuriate in that irony. *Execute.*

Your uncle was accused of having too many animals. All well fed and taken care of. The news report says so. But the neighbors didn't like it. And they didn't like him. The 911 dispatcher was the final call he made. Not an I love you. Or...I'll be home soon. A desperate plea for help to a complete and total stranger.

Listen to him yell, "I ain't committed a crime. Get the fuck out of here! What are you bursting in my house for?"

All true. He hadn't committed a crime. Because technically having cats that are taken care of isn't a crime.

Unless you live in a white, affluent community that objects to you having your back door open so the cats can go outside. Say that again out loud. Leaving the back door open. No, the other part. White affluent community. Fancy way of saying your neighbors can get you killed without getting blood on their hands.

An officer yells for him to come out with his hands up. 27 seconds later they kill him. A TACT team to issue a search warrant? Shake your head. Your hands are shaking. This tactical unit is trained to respond to barricade situations, hostage rescues, counterterrorism, and high-risk felony apprehensions and old white guys with too many cats. This is the exact thing your uncle railed about. People who give power to the police because they don't want to protect themselves.

You listen to him arguing with the police through a door. He sounds confused, almost childlike.

He pleads, "Why are you breaking into my house?"

You already know the answer. Supreme authority rules. And your rich, white neighbors want you dead because you are a nuisance.

You stop to think about why a TACT team waits until night to kick in the door of a 69 year old man who was never officially charged with a crime. You see your cousin crying on the news. He looks so confused, so hurt. His daddy is dead. His daddy is dead. He loved his dad.

The internet is full of news reports. Pages of hits. Scroll. Scroll. It's so overwhelming. Who do you tell? How do you tell them?

Instant Message your husband. It's the only sane thing to do. After shock and a few minutes, a message flashes on the screen: The guy who killed him ran Homeland Security.

"What?" you say, absolutely incredulous.

Then you search the cop who killed him and the first hit is a LinkedIn profile. There he is, smiling big for the world to see. The man who murdered your uncle. We act like it's not murder if the cops do it.

But it is. Taking a life. A life taken.

A grandfather. A father. An uncle. A brother.

He wasn't a saint. You grapple with this fact. But he loved those animals. And he was proud of you. So proud of you.

Go back to the profile. Investigator at the police department. Homeland Security/Counterterrorism. He specializes in high-risk entry. That's a fancy way of saying he'll throw a flash bang into a room and shoot you three times with an M4 rifle.

At close range. High Risk Entry. Mutha fucka.

The high-risk suspect begged 911 to send help. Who were they going to send? That part is kind of a joke, don't you think? No one was coming to help. Help was already there. Close your eyes and repeat that sentence until you believe it.

Your husband Instant Messages and says he just found out his stepfather was arrested for helping drug dealers launder money because he utilizes the same method for dealing with his family that you use. Total avoidance.

He learns his stepfather served six months prison time, then six months house arrest. He's a former jailbird turned snitch. Served on the County Board of Commissioners. He had to wear a wire. Government officials and career criminals are cut from the same cloth.

Then the riots break out in Baltimore.

Really. Because you cannot make this shit up.

You sit stunned into heightened awareness, watching anger on display. The media calls it, "unrest." You snort and lean in close to the monitor like that hack reporter can hear you and whisper, "Burn that mutha fucka down. Burn it down."

It's a mantra. Repeated over the course of days. Burn it down. Not because you wish for people to lose their communities. Not because you don't think life is precious. You chant because the system is broken. Broken so far down the dirt is splintered. Bring that broken system to its knees. Bring it down. Bring it down to its broken, splintered parts and then crush them with your boot.

There's a guy in Baltimore dead. Your uncle is dead. Your husband's stepfather took a plea deal.

You write all of this down in a journal that you bought at the Louisa May Alcott house outside of Boston six months ago. You remember looking out at the ocean from the Boston shore. You think about when your uncle went back to Mississippi and found out his soon to be ex-wife wasn't taking care of the Arabian horses. Divorce was such a nasty word back then. God help us. Her name was Norma Jean.

You remember Boston. Remember the haunted inn where you had dinner. A quaint, charming New England town with squares and roundabouts. Think about how Mexico City is your favorite city in all the world. You're all ADD at this second. Someone has died. Someone is in the ground. You want to call your cousin. The one who told you that your grandmother never got a tombstone because your mom is an ex junkie liar. *Liar liar, pants on fire.*

Focus.

The first time you were in Boston you talked to your uncle. Downtown near Chinatown. You saw a Mongol outside a noodle house. You bought a porcelain Buddha and thought about buying a tea set but how many fucking tea sets does one person need?

Suddenly, you realize that all of your childhood photos were in your uncle's house. The ones your mother left in the garage. You realize they are gone now. Carted out with the contents of his life to the city dump. Humans bury everything. Nothing sacred. Nothing gained.

You remember throwing a pin from Paris off a bridge in North Carolina. Down into the river it went. You were afraid to bury your pain back then. Afraid if you buried it, it would grow. Had to let it go. Let it flow.

A staggering numbness claims your insides. Inside every cell. You can't shake it off. You stare at the hysterical commentators in Baltimore. Watch how a city in crisis is reduced to sound bites.

Take away the jobs. Take away the men. Take away the balance. Gun down everyone who is angry. Your uncle was a Libertarian. He was angry. Thought the government was a dangerous joke. Turns out, he was right.

There's his face. Right there in the newspaper. In a moment of dark tinged snark you realize, like all good Southerners, you learn about what your family is up to on the evening news.

There's a curfew in Baltimore. Your uncle hated that marshal law crap.

You're pretty sure he killed a woman in Arizona and fled the state. You could never prove it. But you suspect it. He wasn't a saint.

Lay in bed with your husband and listen to the Baltimore police scanner. What a long three days. Long and hard. Dead is supposed to be hard. Supposed to wrangle us out of ruts masquerading as comfort zones.

Look at the face of the man who gunned down your uncle. He's right there. He kills people for a living. Hard to get around that fact. License to kill. Your uncle is consistently referred to as a suspect in every news report. Yet he was never charged.

Laying in bed listening to the riots in Baltimore you are suddenly grateful that in the last years of your uncle's life you talked to him constantly for hours on the phone. Your cousin offered to take you to dinner. You got to know him more and more. He admitted that he loved junk and wasn't particularly tidy. That he wasn't the greatest about cleaning up but he loved his animals. He told you his neighbors hated him because he didn't want his lawn manicured and he didn't want to lease an Audi.

The news reports claim there were raccoons and opossums living in the house. It must have been those opossums that made it such a high-risk entry.

You wonder what ever happened to your grandmother's house. The one that has languished into disrepair. You pull it up on Google Earth. There it is. Your childhood home. Emotion floods into your brain. You remember running up that front concrete walk a hundred million times. Maybe a hundred bazillion.

"That's where I grew up," you say to your husband, excited, pointing at the screen.

That was your childhood home. With your fingers you turn the view and travel that dead-end street two houses down where a Chinese artist lived. You remember the time you and your best friend went down and knocked on his door and asked if you could see the inside of his house.

He looked at both of you like you were off your rocker and asked why.

"Because you're an artist," you said confidently because you were sure you wanted to know what the den of an artist looked like.

Because he was awesome and good natured and maybe even a little flattered he took you on a tour of his home while you *ooohed* and *aaaahed* at every tiny thing, especially the fact that his home looked lived in. He got paid for making art. Cash money. He was quite possibly the coolest dude on planet Earth. His house is still there. You have no idea what happened to him.

The National Guard rolls into Baltimore.

The last time you were in Baltimore was November, to see the Snowden documentary Citizen Four. The problems didn't start in one night. Everyone who loves Baltimore knows that. These riots have been a long time coming.

You go downstairs. Sit quietly at your desk. Listen to the 911 call three times. The last thing your uncle said in this world, in this life is, "I don't know if you shot my animals or not." And his voice quivers. And the tape goes dead. And so does he.

It's true he should have lived in Montana on a huge stretch of land. So far out that he didn't have to see anyone. He didn't need the superficial comfort of waving to neighbors or home delivery of mail. He regarded humans as a lot not to be trusted.

That's how he came to live with cats, chickens, dogs, raccoons, and opossums. There were no raccoons and opossums. The neighbors made it up.

Your uncle rescued cats from the pound so they wouldn't be murdered in cold blood. He thought it was wrong. All that killing. So do you.

You could say his love of baby kitties got him killed. You could say it's about race but there is really only one color in the human race. Your true color. The news reports said the neighbors were saddened but relieved they no longer have to live next to him. He collected junk and put it in his backyard. He was a nuisance. Like a rat. His white neighbors are so relieved. After all, they got away with murder. Those zany white neighbors.

The man who gunned down your uncle has his own website.

His company's team is fluent in English, Spanish, and Hebrew.

He specializes in mitigating threats.

His birthday is December 28.

You can send him a request to connect.

Praise for other Titles

The Wonder Years meets Christmas Story meets E.T. in this magical novel...

Cathy Smith Bowers
Former Poet Laureate of North Carolina, and South Carolina Author's Hall of Fame Inductee

Gobbledy

"Hugely entertaining as well as emotionally moving."

—Kirkus Reviews

"This charming alien-in-the-attic story boasts engaging characters, witty storytelling, and a furry little beast that will eat anything, all wrapped up in a warm holiday package."

—Booklife

"A delightfully entertaining novel by an author with a genuine flair for originality and the kind of narrative storytelling style that will fully engage the imaginative attention of appreciative young readers ages 8-11, Gobbledy by Lis Anna-Langston ... will prove to be an immediate and enduringly popular addition to elementary school, middle school, and community library collections."

—Midwest Book Review

Tupelo Honey

A loveable, engaging, original voice, Tupelo brightens this accomplished tale of dysfunction in a family where "nothing had ever been right.".

~ Publishers Weekly ~

From the delicious title (the spunky 11-year-old narrator was named after Elvis' birthplace) to every last unconventional character and careful detail, Tupelo Honey is a delight. Set in rural Mississippi, with a cast of colorful southerners, it stars one pretty dysfunctional family at the center of which is Tupelo Honey. Author Lis Anna-Langston gets into the head of her title girl completely, taking readers on a ride of a sort of haunted but beautiful mess.

It's certainly not a dull life, one full of heartbreaks big and small, but this tough sweet girl pulls it off with aplomb. It's a treat from start to end. Langston has written rich, vivid characters, and painted a vibrant mosaic of a year in one young southern girl's life. It's a hard book to put down, and one you won't want to end. I envy its future readers.

~ Teresa DiFalco ©2016 Parents' Choice ~

Maya Loop

"Maya Loop is Alice in Wonderland meets the Wizard of Oz, with the sweet tinge of Fortnite and Percy Jackson thrown in. I loved every page."

- Linda Sands, Award winning Georgia Author of the Year

Readers interested in a passionate journey of determination and evolving wisdom will find Maya Loop unpredictable, driven by understandable emotions and extraordinary events that lead Maya to a new form of determination and courage.

- D. Donovan, Senior Reviewer, Midwest Book Review

Acknowledgements

Books don't form in a vacuum. This collection is the result of years of classes and workshops. These short stories were all individually published in literary journals and magazines. This is the first time publishing the entire collection as a book.

I would like to acknowledge and thank each Editor who chose my work for publication and in some instances, worked with me on the manuscript. Great Editors are tireless champions of literature and every second spent with one makes me a better writer. I am also deeply grateful for the audiences I reached in each publication. The gift of an audience to an Author is the greatest gift of all.

"Tips" and "Roommates" were nominated for a Pushcart
"The Descent" won Second Place in the Thomas Wolfe Fiction Awards
"Vegas Thunder" won the Readers Choice Award
"Roommates" won the Editors Choice Award and was nominated for Best of the Web.

For all of the nominations and wins I am deeply awed by the spirit and attention of the literary community.

A big thank you to J. Thomas Meador who is just about the best workshopping partner I could ever have.

A huge thanks to my husband who edits and proofs all of my manuscripts. He is my biggest fan and encourages all of my insanity. His attention to me and my work makes a difference. I love him wonderfully.

And to all of the participants, in all of the workshops and classes, over the years, I am grateful to have listened to your stories, even more grateful you listened to mine.

List of publications with citations

"The Dollhouse." Petigru Review Volume 1, 2007
"Figs." The Smoking Poet Winter 2009-2010 Issue 13
"Plastic." Eclectic Flash Literary Journal April 2010, Volume 1
"Roommates." Fiction Fix Issue 9, Spring 2011, Pushcart nomination
"The Descent." The Monarch Review Winter April 12, 2011
"You Are Such A Poem." 5x5 Literary Magazine Summer 2011, Illumination
"Abandon." Red Booth Review May 2011, Issue 23
"Twelve Drawers." Emyrs Journal Volume 29, 2012
"Vegas Thunder." Literary Laundry, Volume 2, Issue 1, Autumn 2011
"The Temp." Barely South Review April 2012, Old Dominion University
"Tolstoy & the Checkout Girl" Barely South Review September 2012, Old Dominion University
"Tips." Steel Toe Review Volume 3, 2013 Pushcart nomination
"Dirty Nickel." The Ottawa Object Volume 2, 2016
"A Feeling." The Merrimack Review Winter 2014-2015, Issue Two
"The End of the Century." The Sand Hill Review Summer 2015, Volume 16
"sex. with kerouac." Prick of the Spindle, A Journal of the Literary Arts, Vol. 5.3, Sept. 2011
"86 Miles from El Paso." The MacGuffin, Winter 2007, Volume XXIII, No. 2
"Abandon." The MacGuffin, Winter 2007, Volume XXIII, No. 2
"The Day You Find Out Your Uncle Was Gunned Down by Police." Conclave, Spring 2016

ABOUT THE AUTHOR

LIS ANNA-LANGSTON was raised alongside the winding current of the Mississippi River on a steady diet of dog-eared books. Thrice nominated for the Pushcart, the award-winning author of Gobbledy & Tupelo Honey loves ketchup, starry skies, chinchillas, French hip hop & stories with happy aliens.

You can find her in the wilds of South Carolina plucking stories out of thin air.

Subscribe to her Life on the Lis(t)
@
www.lisannalangston.com